DEADLY FLASH FROM THE PAST

A WHISPERING HAVEN COZY MYSTERY

RUTH BAKER

CLEANTALES PUBLISHING

Copyright © CleanTales Publishing

First published in October 2024

All characters and events in this publication, other than those clearly in the public domain, are fictitious and any resemblance to real persons, living or dead, is purely coincidental.

Copyright © CleanTales Publishing

The moral right of the author has been asserted.

All rights reserved. This book or any portion thereof may not be reproduced or used in any manner whatsoever without the express written permission of the publisher except for the use of brief quotations in a book review.

For questions and comments about this book, please contact info@cleantales.com

ISBN: 9798344448275
Imprint: Independently Published

OTHER BOOKS IN THE WHISPERING HAVEN SERIES

Gone in a Snap

Say Cheese and Die Laughing

Deadly Flash from the Past

Framed in Mischief

Blurred Lines, Clear Crimes

Snap, Crackle and a Deadly Plot

Flash of Deceit

A Whispering Haven Cozy Mystery

BOOK THREE

CHAPTER 1

The sun beat down, warming the bench as Carol and Harriet lounged in the park, watching the passersby.

"It's days like this when I remember why I can never move back to Phoenix," Carol sighed, leaning her back against the bench. "If we were there right now, it would probably be over a hundred degrees. I never could stand the heat."

"I know, right?" Harriet said. The light through the trees spread dappled patterns across her skin and face, making the scattering of grey in her brown hair gleam almost silver. "I haven't looked back since I moved here eight months ago." She gave a comical shiver. "Though I miss those Georgia winters."

"No kidding. After living in Phoenix nearly my whole life, I didn't realize it could get this cold," Carol admitted. "Still, it's been nice, and I definitely enjoy the people here." She nudged Harriet. "Present company included."

Carol and Harriet had met a few weeks ago, while Carol had been photographing a wedding for a couple. They had run into one another at the drink table and started chatting, which eventually devolved to swapping photos of their cats and gardens, cooing over the kittens and getting into a spirited debate about the best way to combat pests, before Carol hurriedly ran to photograph the cake cutting.

"You're too sweet," Harriet said, beaming. She stood, stretching her back. "Do you want to go walk down by the harbor? It's a gorgeous day."

"As long as you don't mind my stopping every few minutes to take photos," Carol retorted, also standing. "It's too perfect a day to leave this thing just dangling around my neck."

They started wandering through downtown, enjoying the oceanside town, the wooden buildings stained with saltwater and old docks covered in barnacles dotting the waters. Restaurants with ocean views were filled with tourists and locals alike, all enjoying their lunch in the quaint Maine town.

Whispering Haven really did feel like that: a haven. Carol had been there for over a year now, and it still felt like a paradise whenever she wandered its streets. Though that might have been because, for the first several months, she'd been a bit of a hermit, grieving over the sudden death of her husband, Robert. It hadn't been until Sarah Jean had dragged her out of her house that she had truly started coming out of her shell, starting to take professional photos for weddings and other events.

Though maybe the real reason she had managed to come out of her shell was only tangentially related to photography. Maybe it had more to do with her other side job, one that came about sporadically, but one she secretly yearned to do more of.

That, of course, was solving murders with her pseudo-partner, Paul.

There was something thrilling about uncovering secrets and plots, about putting criminals behind bars. It gave her a rush of adrenaline that she hadn't experienced anywhere else, and it gave her a sense of purpose she had yet to receive from anything else, though photography came close.

As her mind drifted toward this, she had a bit of an itch, the kind she only experienced when she thought about her side job. She needed to call Paul and see if there had been anything else. Last time, Tex had promised that if there was a new investigation he thought they could help with, he would let them know. She'd scoured the papers. So far, however, she hadn't read of any murder or mysterious death since her last case.

Which, for Whispering Haven, was a good thing, even if, in her own mind, it was a little disappointing. She knew she shouldn't be wishing for another murder, but the thrill of solving cases gave her a rush of adrenaline like nothing else she had experienced.

She pushed those thoughts from her mind as they cleared the old wooden buildings of downtown and opened onto a stunning view of the harbor and the cerulean ocean beyond.

The harbor was filled with the sound of seagulls and boats moving in and out. Further out to sea, boats dotted the horizon as they bobbed in the water. The wind carried the salt air, blowing their hair and stinging their faces. It was the type of tableau that photographers dreamed of. Carol slowed, pulled out her camera, and began snapping, trying to catch the way the light shone off the hulls of the boats and the glistening water.

"It's lovely out here," Harriet said. She pointed to one of the boats. "Oh! I didn't know they had whale tour boats here. We should do one sometime."

"That would be fun!" Carol said. Then, more to herself, she mused, "I wonder if Sarah Jean would like something like that. She's been here a long time, so maybe she's already done it."

"What about Sarah Jean?" Harriet asked. "You two are friends, aren't you? Did I hear someone say she had a birthday coming up?"

"Next week." Carol's smile faltered, and she bit her lip. "That's one of the only problems," she said. "I have no idea what to get Sarah Jean for her birthday. She always seemed like the type of person who gets what she wants whenever she wants it."

Harriet nodded. "I don't know Sarah Jean super well, but I see what you mean."

"You two would get along really well, actually," Carol mused. "I should have you both over for coffee sometime."

Harriet grinned. "You mean I get to go to your house and spoil Buttons? That sounds awful."

Carol laughed. "Buttons doesn't need any more spoiling.

She's already so pampered that she's getting a huge ego over it."

"She's a cat. Being full of themselves is part of the job description."

They continued walking, following the weathered wooden planks along the harbor, Carol turned, gasping with delight when she saw Harriet in between two posts, the old but well-maintained lighthouse directly to her right.

"Oh, here!" Carol whipped out her camera. "Stay right there. You're framed perfectly."

Harriet blushed, then began posing, giving ridiculous, silly poses mixed in with genuine sweet photos where she gave a radiant smile.

"These all look wonderful," Carol exclaimed, looking at the camera and flicking through the photos, eyes glinting as she scrutinized each photo. "You're so photogenic, Harriet."

"Flatterer," Harriet said, color rising to her cheeks. "You're too sweet."

"I'm being serious," Carol argued. She marched over to her friend, practically shoving the camera in her face. "See? Look at this one. You look fantastic. The camera loves you!"

Harriet laughed, eyes crinkling as she took the camera gingerly from Carol. The laughter froze on her face as she looked at the photo. The joy melted away as Harriet's features turned waxen, her eyes somber. She looked as though she'd aged twenty years in five seconds.

She whipped her head around, her lips thin, a stricken

expression on her face as her eyes darted everywhere, as if searching for something.

"Is everything all right?" Carol asked, frowning. "Is there something wrong with the photo?"

"No...no..." Harriet murmured, as if she'd barely heard Carol. Her fingers trembled as she passed the camera back to Carol. "Everything's fine. I just..." She coughed, as if trying to choke out the words even as she kept staring out, searching for something that Carol couldn't see. "I've got to go."

"Is something wrong?" Carol asked, brow furrowed. "I'm sorry. I didn't mean to offend you. I thought it was a really nice photo."

She glanced at the photo that had apparently given her friend a panic attack, confusion still rippling through her. Something had triggered in Harriet in the span of a few seconds, and Carol had no idea what had happened.

Harriet gave a strained smile, one that didn't reach her eyes. "It's a lovely photo, Carol," she promised. "But right now, I really have to get going. There's something I need to do."

She gave Carol a quick, reassuring hug, and then ran off, leaving Carol standing in the middle of the sidewalk, staring after her friend in bewilderment and concern.

CHAPTER 2

Carol chewed her lip, scowling as her mind reeled and she stared down at her list of potential birthday gifts. None of them seemed to work for Sarah Jean. What would she do with an air fryer? And gift cards always felt so impersonal.

She huffed. It was times like this when she really missed Robert. He'd always been the one good at birthday presents. If he were here, he'd make a casual suggestion that would turn out to be perfect. It had been over a year, but it still ached when she thought about him. Instances like this made his absence that much more apparent.

She reached for her cup of coffee, hoping the caffeine would give her a needed boost. Before she could, however, a grey shorthair hopped onto the kitchen table, pushing herself between Carol and the mug to rub against Carol's face, purring as she did.

"Good morning to you, too, Buttons," Carol said, laughing

as Button's tail flicked affectionately off Carol's face. "Though I'm pretty sure I told you not to get on the table."

Buttons blinked at Carol, her purr growing louder. She plopped on the table and sprawled out, stretching and indicating in no uncertain terms that she had no intention of going anywhere.

"You're lucky you're cute," Carol said, without a hint of animosity. Buttons licked her paw before swiping it across her forehead.

Carol's mind went to Harriet the day before. She'd seemed so upset when she had looked at the photo. No, upset wasn't quite the right word. She'd seemed worried. She wished Harriet had confided in her. Something had really bothered her. But she had no idea what or why. Her intuition screamed at her that Harriet, if not in trouble, was certainly in distress. She needed to talk to her, to see if Harriet needed someone to confide in. Even if she didn't want to, she could at least let Harriet know there was someone in her corner if she needed help.

She dialed Harriet's number and held it up to her ear, waiting. The tone rang out, but ultimately switched to voicemail.

Unease growing and squirming in her stomach, she lowered the phone, idly reaching out to scratch Buttons behind the ears. A disquiet washed over her as she wondered what could have happened. Something wasn't right. Her curiosity flared, and she made a promise to herself to figure out what was going on and to help her friend at all costs.

What if it had something to do with the photo? She couldn't imagine what it had been that had upset her so much that she had run off, but it was the only thing that made any logical sense.

Maybe if she took another look at those photos, she could get a better idea of what was going on. She went over to the computer, hooking her camera up to transfer over the photos. That was one good thing about getting into photography. Over the last few months, she had gotten a lot more tech savvy than she'd been previously.

Pulling up the photos, she flicked through each of the ones of Harriet, lingering on the one she had shown her friend. On the surface, she couldn't pick out anything concerning or amiss. It simply looked like Harriet was having a fun day out and goofing off for the camera. Carol couldn't imagine Harriet being that upset with her appearance—she was stunning in the photo and, even then, she had never seemed the type to get so upset about a picture that she would run off without explanation. No, it had to be something else. Perhaps something in the background.

As she continued examining the photos she'd shown Harriet, her confidence began to wane. Nothing stood out to her. What if she'd been wrong about the whole thing? Pushing those thoughts to the side, she kept going.

She paused, cursor hovering over a figure in the background. He had a gruff face, rugged stubble and a harsh mouth. His hair suggested he was in his mid-forties, but the leathery skin suggested someone far older. He was squinting into the camera. No, not into the camera. He was squinting at Harriet.

She zoomed in on his face. His eyes were narrowed, his lips turned into what looked like a scowl. Still, there was something handsome about his features at the same time. He had the type of face that looked as though it would be charming when he smiled. More than charming, radiant. She could imagine him melting hearts if he had the mind to. She moved down, looking at the rest of the man.

No paunch. For middle-aged, he looked surprisingly fit. As her eyes drifted down, she paused as she locked onto his hands, a cold sense of unease crawling through her body.

His fingers were clenched into fists.

She glanced back at his face, that glare that seemed to dig into Harriet's back. She wasn't imagining it, then. He looked legitimately furious. The icy rage boiling in him was unmistakable. He knew Harriet. And based on Harriet's reaction, she knew him. But who was he?

As she pondered this, her phone rang, breaking her concentration and startling her. Her surprise quickly gave way to excitement, however, when she saw who was calling. Paul Morris, a private detective and her partner. She sucked in a breath. There's only one reason why he would be calling.

"Paul!" she exclaimed when she answered. "Good to hear from you."

"Heya," Paul said.

"Well?" she asked expectantly.

"Well what?" he teased.

"Are you calling because we've got a case or because you're bored?" she retorted.

DEADLY FLASH FROM THE PAST

A rumble of amused laughter rippled through the phone. "We've got a case," Paul said. "Assuming you're interested."

Carol leaped to her feet, startling Buttons, who had been curled up on the couch.

"Of course I'm interested," she said, not bothering to hide her excitement. "What is it?"

"Dead body at the harbor."

Despite the grimness and macabre of the situation, despite her concerns about Harriet, excitement rippled through her, practically giddy. "I'll head out now."

Wanting to get to the harbor quickly, she made the rare decision to take her car. She raced to her car, then stopped and doubled back to grab her forgotten camera. Forcing herself not to drive like a maniac, she hurried to the harbor.

It didn't take a genius to figure out where the body was. Yellow police tape roped off a portion of walkway, and uniformed officers wandered around inside, muttering in clusters.

Carol clambered out of her car, looking around. A tall man, his dark hair lightly salted with gray, strolled up, hands in his pockets.

"Carol, good to see you," Paul said, his green eyes crinkling.

"You, too." She eyed the cluster of officers hovering around a body she couldn't see. "Are we going to have trouble with the police again?" she asked, nodding to the group. Memories of some of her previous encounters with the police made her uneasy. It often involved them taking her camera and refusing to give it back for several days.

"Not if I have anything to say about it," an unfamiliar voice said. Carol turned to see another familiar face strutting toward them. The sun glinted off a bronze badge in the shape of a star pinned to his chest. He gave a small smile and a nod for a greeting. "I told the guys you're here on a consulting basis. If any of them give you any trouble, come to me."

"Appreciate it, Tex," Paul said, nodding at the broad-shouldered sheriff. "In that case, let's take a look."

"So what do you know?" Carol asked as they marched over.

"We've got a bit of a doozy," Paul said. "Tourist. As far as we can tell, he was in Whispering Haven alone, only we don't know why he was here. No clear motive at the moment, either."

Tex held up the bright yellow tape so Carol and Paul could dip beneath it.

"A woman called in the body a couple of hours ago," Tex explained. "We've got a lot of questions we've got left to answer, so be mindful while you're trying to look over things, all right? Hey, you guys, clear the way."

The officers huddled together glanced up. They glanced from Tex to the two newcomers in plainclothes. An air of confusion lingered over the group as they surveyed them, but after a moment, they stepped aside, letting them pass. Another couple of steps, and she could see the body, sightless eyes staring up at the clear blue sky.

She came to a halt the instant the body came into view. Her hand flew to her mouth, eyes growing wide with shock.

"I know him," she said.

Tex and Paul's heads whipped around to stare at her in surprise.

"You do?" Paul asked.

"How?" Tex said. "He isn't local."

"I know," Carol said, eyes still locked on the man's face, one she'd seen minutes before dashing to the car. "He was following me yesterday."

It was the man from the photo.

CHAPTER 3

"He was *following* you?" Tex asked, bewildered.

"Sort of. I took a photo with him in it yesterday," she said. "Actually, he was in a few of them. I was going through my pictures this morning and I thought it was strange."

She didn't add Harriet's strange reaction to seeing him. She wanted to keep that to herself until it became important. The last thing she wanted was to implicate her friend. Harriet deserved a phone call first, at least. If she could give a good explanation, then she didn't see the need to tell Tex or Paul. At least not yet. Hopefully, she wouldn't have to.

"You think he was following you?" Tex drawled, raising a brow in interest.

"I don't know," Carol said. "I just noticed he was in a couple of my photos. I didn't even notice him when I was out and about. But I don't know…this feels a little too coincidental."

Tex nodded.

"You can't think of a reason he would be trailing you?" Paul asked. When Carol shook her head, he gave her a speculative look, as if he could tell she wasn't being entirely honest. She tried to communicate back silently that she would explain everything later. She wasn't sure he understood entirely, but he did give a brief nod, promising he wouldn't prod further right then.

"We'll need to see those photos," Tex said, oblivious to the silent conversation between her and her partner.

"I can get them to you tomorrow," Carol promised. *That will give me enough time to talk to Harriet and see if she can give me any answers*, she thought.

"What do you know about him?" Carol asked.

"Out of towner," Paul said. "His ID says he's James Ratfield, from Atlanta."

"Georgia?"

Paul's brow furrowed. "I don't know of any other Atlantas," he said.

She tried to keep her face impassive, but she could practically feel the color draining from her face. Georgia. Where Harriet was from. Again, Carol thought back to Harriet's reaction to the photo. It had been one that resembled both horror and recognition, as if she knew who the man was, and was terrified of him.

What kind of person would elicit that sort of reaction from the sweet, mild-mannered Harriet? It couldn't be a coincidence that he had been from Georgia. Did that mean they knew one another before Harriet moved? There was no telling. Still, unease crept up her spine. She needed to talk to Harriet, and fast.

She pushed those thoughts from her mind. She needed to focus on the present if she were going to be of any help. She started snapping photos.

"How did he die?" Carol asked, as she continued to click away.

"Gun shot," Tex said.

"We haven't been able to find the murder weapon yet, though," Paul said.

"We're dredging the harbor to see if the killer threw it out there," Tex said. "Also running ballistics on the bullets."

"Plural?"

Tex nodded. "Shot three times," he explained.

"You want to know the interesting bit?" Paul asked.

"I want to know *all* the bits," Carol fired back. "The interesting and the boring."

Paul grinned. "Atta girl," he said, nodding. "Speaking with the coroner—" he jerked his head in the direction of a balding man removing latex gloves and muttering to himself — "Just one of those bullets would have been enough to kill Ratfield. Skilled marksman type deal."

"So why shoot him three times?" Carol mused.

Paul tapped the side of his nose in a *you got it* type gesture. "Odds are, he really wanted to make sure the guy was dead, or it was personal."

Carol tried to keep her expression blank, but already her heart hammered with unease. Personal. Meaning someone who knew him. She thought back to that horrified look of recognition on Harriet's face when she had seen the photo, the way she had run off. It had certainly seemed as though she knew who the man was. But did that mean she was the one who killed him?

No, certainly not. Harriet wasn't the type of person who could murder someone in cold blood. Could she?

Back at home, Carol tapped the phone nervously against her thigh, staring down at the carpet as she debated what to do. She needed to talk to Harriet, to see if there was some connection, but she didn't know how to broach the subject.

She paced back and forth as she chewed her lip, mind spinning with thoughts and ways to approach the touchy subject. But how could she?

Buttons, seeing her human in distress, meowed and followed at her heel, looking up occasionally, obviously wondering why Carol was walking back and forth on the carpet when snoozing on the couch was a much more comfortable option. She wound her way between Carol's legs, threatening to trip her.

The rest of the time at the crime scene had gone by in a blur. There hadn't been much more information to go off of by the time she left. No sign of the murder weapon, no clues as to why he was there. The only real piece of information they obtained was they found an old-fashioned room key tucked in his pocket, one for The Seaport Bed and

Breakfast. She and Paul had plans to check it out in a day or so. But, for now, she had other pressing things to deal with.

Like figuring out the connection between Harriet and the now-deceased James Ratfield.

Taking a deep breath, she dialed her friend and waited.

"Carol! Hi!" Harriet said after two rings. "I'm so sorry about missing your call. Eric and I were out at brunch. And I'm sorry about yesterday, too. I just realized I had forgotten something at home, and I needed to take care of it before something happened. "

"That's fine," Carol said.

"What can I do for you?" Harriet chirped. "Are you looking for someone to grab brunch with? I was actually going to ask your advice on some gardening tips, so that would be perfect."

"I...actually wanted to talk to you about yesterday," Carol admitted, still not sure how to approach any of this. "I went back and looked through the photos. I noticed a man there."

A pause filled the air as Carol waited.

"I'm sorry. I don't follow," Harriet finally said, the joy in her voice subsiding, her tone going flat.

"I wanted to ask if he was the reason you ran off," Carol said, still tiptoeing around the real issue at hand. "When you looked at the photo, it seemed as though you'd seen a ghost. It's really important. If he had something to do with it...if he frightened you—"

"What?" Harriet tittered. "Carol, that's silly. I told you I just realized I had to run home. It didn't have anything to do with some guy in the photos. But I really appreciate your concern."

"You would tell me if you did, right?" Carol asked.

"Naturally."

"You promise? Because it really seems like you know him. And I need you to answer truthfully. It's really important."

"Carol, honestly, now, this is ridiculous. You're making assumptions you know nothing about." An almost hostile edge had entered her voice, her hackles beginning to rise. "And even if I did know him—which I don't—what does it matter? It's my business. Not yours."

"Harriet," Carol said, her voice surprisingly firm. "I don't think you understand. The man in the photo, he was found dead this morning."

Silence.

"What?" Harriet asked, her voice strained.

"His name was James Ratfield," Carol explained. "Are you sure that name doesn't mean anything to you?"

"No, no. I've never heard that name before in my life," Harriet claimed. Something about the rapid denial made Carol wonder if she was telling the truth.

The more they spoke, the more dread built in her stomach, the more certain she was that Harriet was keeping something from her, something imperative to the investigation.

"So it was all a coincidence?" Carol asked, giving her friend one more chance to recant and tell the truth.

DEADLY FLASH FROM THE PAST

"As far as I know," Harriet said. "Look, Carol, I really appreciate you asking and checking on me, but I'm fine, really. I don't know anything about a James Ratling—"

"Ratfield."

"That just proves my point. I don't know anything about any of this. I'm really sorry, but I've got to run. I've got a lot of errands to run. I'll talk to you later, all right?"

"Harriet, wait—"

"Bye!"

Harriet hung up, leaving Carol with nothing but a dial tone and even more questions.

One thing was certain: Harriet wasn't telling her the whole truth. And she needed to find out why.

CHAPTER 4

Carol paced back and forth in her garden, enjoying the summer air and the scent of flowers as she contemplated the wild events that had happened over the past day. Nearby, Buttons lounged in a sunny spot in the green grass, sprawled out as she watched the birds flying overhead. A butterfly fluttered close to her, and the cat reached out a grey paw and swatted lazily as it breezed past.

Carol bit her nails as worries about Harriet swelled inside her. She knew something wasn't right. Her intuition screamed at her that she needed to step in and do something, that Harriet was in trouble. But if Harriet wouldn't confide in her, then she had no way of knowing or helping.

Should she call her again?

"Hello?" a familiar voice broke through Carol's musings. She spun around to see Sarah Jean leaning over the gate and flicking open the latch and letting herself in.

"Sarah Jean?"

"Of course! You didn't forget, did you?"

Forget? Forget what? It wasn't her birthday yet, was it? It was next week, right? Just as the panic began to swell in her chest and she scrambled to formulate an apology, her eyes caught on the plastic bag clutched in Sarah Jean's hand, and she relaxed, breathing a sigh of relief.

"Apparently, I have," she joked.

Sarah Jean gave a mock scoff, the fake lecture diminished by the sparkle in her eyes. "Well, I certainly hope you've remembered your part of the bargain. Otherwise these—" She shook the plastic bag, where several seeds rattled and hopped with the motion. "—are coming back with me." She winked.

Carol laughed. "Don't worry, don't worry. I collected mine a couple of days ago."

Stretching her back, she jerked her head toward her back door and moved that way, Sarah Jean hurrying to trot next to her.

"I've heard you've had an interesting twenty-four hours," Sarah Jean said with a singsong lilt. Carol raised her eyebrow.

"How on earth do you know that already?" she demanded, holding the door open for her friend.

"A little birdie or two told me," she said. "Though I would have preferred to have heard it from you," she added in a mock-lecture that made Carol chuckle.

"Well, next time, I'll be sure to remember that," she promised, walking over to a drawer. "In the meantime..." She opened the drawer and pulled out a bag resting on top. Pulling it out, she rattled the bag, the seeds inside softly clacking against one another.

Sarah Jean let out an almost girlish squeal as she clapped her hands together. She snatched the bag from Carol's hands and clutched them to her chest, holding them as though they might vanish if she loosened her grip.

"Thank you!" she said, bouncing on the balls of her feet. "I've been envious of your white roses for months now."

"And I've been wanting to get my hands on your tomatoes for ages," Carol retorted, looking at the small collection of seeds in the bag Sarah Jean had brought. "Granted, I'll have to wait a while before planting them, but now that I have them, I'll be able to plan for next year.

"I just love the idea of a seed swap," Sarah Jean said, examining her newly acquired seeds. "This was such a good idea, Carol."

"It benefits both of us," Carol said.

Sarah Jean tapped her finger against her chin, mulling something over.

"You know, I wonder if maybe we should try and do a neighborhood-wide swap," she mused. "I know for a fact that there would be some other women around here interested in doing it. Mary's been begging for my tulips for years."

"I think that's a wonderful idea," Carol said. "I'm still a bit of a hermit at times, even when I don't mean to be. This would be a great way for me to get out and about more often, and meet some of the other gardeners." She walked over to the kettle and held it up. "Do you want some tea?" she asked.

"Of course!"

The two chatted idly while Carol fixed the tea, catching up, Carol surreptitiously attempting to get some information from her friend on what she might like for her birthday. However, Sarah Jean gave nothing away as they talked.

"By the way," Sarah Jean added, nursing the tea now clutched in her hand. "How's Harriet doing?"

Carol blinked. "How do you know there's something wrong?" she asked.

Sarah Jean gasped, eyes flying wide open. "So there is something going on?" she marveled.

"Where did you hear any of this?"

Sarah Jean clicked her teeth, her finger tapping the side of her cup. "Well, I didn't know whether or not to believe it, because it came from Fiona, and you know how she can be."

Carol groaned, closing her eyes. "Of course," Fiona was Whispering Haven's most notorious gossip. She wasn't a bad person by any means, but her propensity for spreading juicy tidbits and rumors could cause unnecessary problems when she wasn't careful. And she normally wasn't. She had her finger on just about everything in town and felt the need to spill others' secrets as much as she needed to absorb them.

"What did she say?" Carol asked.

DEADLY FLASH FROM THE PAST

Buttons hopped on the table, stretching first one way, and then the other, mouth open in a gaping yawn, before curling up on the table between the two women, within perfect distance to receive pets from both women. Sarah Jean reached out idly and began scratching Buttons behind the ears with manicured nails.

"The other day, Fiona was saying that she overheard from someone that her husband was involved in some shady things—"

"*Husband?*" Carol's brow furrowed. "You mean boyfriend. And you know Eric, he feels guilty swatting a mosquito. There's no way he's involved in anything shady."

"I meant husband," Sarah Jean said, eyebrows waggling. She leaned forward, as if worried Buttons would overhear and spread the gossip, even though Buttons was perfectly capable of hearing from her vantage point between them, though her comprehension skills made it safe to discuss anything.

Carol let the words sink in, her mouth partly open in surprise. "She was *married?*" she asked.

"That's what Fiona said." Sarah Jean sat back in her chair. "She said apparently he was a known con man. Harriet left him when she started feeling unsafe. Apparently, a lot of his cons went wrong."

"When did she leave him?" Carol asked. Sarah Jean shrugged. "She never mentioned a husband to me."

Sarah Jean arched an eyebrow. "Not everyone here has a paragon of a husband like you did," she pointed out. "If she moved all the way from Georgia up to Maine, it definitely feels like she wanted to get away from something."

"I moved from Phoenix," Carol pointed out.

With a dismissive flap of her hand, Sarah Jean said, "Regardless, it seemed like Harriet might be in a spot of trouble, so I wanted to know if you knew anything."

Carol bit her lip. "I'm not sure," she admitted. "There's some weird stuff going on, and it ties in with the investigation, but I don't know anything for certain, so I don't want to say anything and accidentally get her in trouble."

Her friend gave a disappointed sigh, even as she nodded. "I get it, even if I'm dying for the gossip," she grumbled. "Especially if it has to do with a body."

"What I want to know is where on earth Fiona gets her information." Carol shook her head. "I swear, it's like she has a sixth sense for these things. I know Harriet never would have told her."

"There's always a chance she's wrong," Sarah Jean pointed out.

Carol flung her hands in the air. "That's the thing, though! She's always right! Remember the time when she started saying Abigail was seeing James from the hardware store? No one would have seen that one coming."

"Body language?" Sarah Jean suggested.

Carol looked her friend dead in the eye. "She managed to find out that my niece and my cousin's kid had a fight because my cousin's daughter accused my niece of stealing her wedding cake design. I didn't tell you that, and I didn't talk about it anywhere but here on the phone."

Sarah Jean blinked, head tilted as she considered. Buttons glanced up, grabbing onto Sarah's hand when she stopped her pets.

"All right, so there's something strange going on there," Sarah Jean said.

"My theory is she has the whole town bugged."

"I still say it's super powers."

The two women lapsed into giggles, cut off only when a loud buzzing sound resonated through the table and Carol's phone lit up. She gasped as she saw the name on the screen: Harriet.

"I've got to take this." She snatched the phone from the table and took a few steps away before answering. "Harriet? I've been trying to reach you for a while. I'm worried about you is everything—"

"Hi, Carol." The masculine voice made Carol stop in bewilderment. "This is Eric, uh, Harriet's boyfriend."

"I know who you are," Carol said. "What's wrong? Why are you using Harriet's phone?"

"Because I need your help, and I don't have your number." The strain in his voice made Carol's own stomach twist into a knot. "Are you working on that new case?"

"Yes," Carol said, her dread growing. "Tex called Paul and I in."

"That's what I thought," Eric sighed. "I—we really need your help."

"Of course. Eric, what happened? What's wrong?"

A pause that seemed to last a lifetime loomed over the phone. Carol could hear her heart thundering. Finally, Eric spoke.

"Harriet's been arrested for murder."

CHAPTER 5

Carol scrambled out of her car and marched toward the police station, feet pounding the pavement as she set a pace that would make an Olympic sprinter jealous. Her heart thundered as she bristled, both with indignation and panic.

She was still reeling from Eric's phone call. Harriet arrested? It seemed unfathomable. And yet, at the same time, it also made perfect sense. Harriet had been cagey when Carol had tried to get information out of her. She clearly had something to hide. However, Carol never would have expected that whatever secret her friend had been hiding would have resulted in her arrest.

Though Eric hadn't given her much in the way of explanation, she knew it had something to do with the murder at the harbor. What else would it be? It would explain her bizarre behavior and panic.

Regardless of her fears and concerns, she needed to focus. Harriet needed her help, and she couldn't let her friend down. So she stomped up to the station, bristling, preparing for a fight. She'd take it all the way to Tex, if she needed.

Just as she stuck her hand out to yank the handle and jerk open the door, it opened from the inside. A tired-looking Harriet and a handsome, middle-aged man with his arm wrapped around her stood on the other side.

"Harriet!" Carol flung her arms around her friend. "Are you all right?"

"I'm fine," Harriet muttered through a sniffle. "Well, as fine as I can be, all things considered."

Carol stepped back, taking in her friend. She looked drawn and withered, as if she had shrunk in on herself.

"What happened?" she demanded. "Eric told me you were arrested."

Harriet sighed, glancing over at Eric. He shrugged.

"She's the best person for this type of job. You know that as well as I do. She's got ins with the police and she's helped solve cases before. I didn't know who else to call for help, and I wasn't going to sit by and do nothing."

Harriet's features softened as she looked at her boyfriend. She leaned against him, taking reassurance from his presence.

"You're so sweet," she muttered. "How did I get so lucky?"

He kissed her forehead. "You can thank me by letting Carol help you."

The softness in Harriet's features hardened for a moment, a panicked, uneasy look washing over her. It seemed obvious to Carol that she still had reservations. Except Eric was right. If Carol was going to help at all, she needed to hear the whole story from Harriet.

But in front of the police station, right after Harriet had just been released, wasn't the right place to have this type of discussion.

"I'm starving," Carol said. "How would you two feel about some lunch at The Pelican?"

The Pelican, a local seafood restaurant that catered more to locals than tourists, looked out over the harbor and ocean. As their hostess seated them on the deck, Carol wondered if maybe her choice hadn't been the wisest. Just on the edge of their view, she could just make out yellow police tape roping off a small portion of the harbor.

"Um...maybe this isn't the best place after all," Carol said. "Their crab cakes aren't *that* good."

Harriet seemed to know exactly what was on her friend's mind and gave a reassuring smile.

"It's fine, Carol," she said. "But I appreciate the concern. It's sweet."

Still, Carol's face flushed, and she was grateful when the waiter materialized a few moments later and took their drink order.

"All right," Carol said, once the waiter had wandered over to his next table. She leaned forward on her forearms, lacing her fingers together as she focused on Harriet. "What's going on? Why were you arrested? How do you know James Ratfield and why did he frighten you so much?"

Harriet hesitated, color flooding her cheeks as she glanced down at the table. Her eyes drifted out to the ocean, drifting, then lingering on the area where Carol knew Harriet could see the yellow tape. Finally, Harriet sighed, her shoulders slumping, and she looked back at Carol.

"I did know James..." she finally admitted. Eric's hand reached out, enveloping Harriet's and giving it a reassuring squeeze. "He is...was my ex-husband."

Out of anything Harriet could have said, this was the one that surprised Carol the most. She blinked, leaning backward as she looked at her friend.

"Really?" Carol asked.

Giving a short jerk of a nod, Harriet took another deep breath, then continued. "He's the reason I left Georgia in the first place. We divorced about two years ago. But even after I divorced him, he kept stalking me. He wouldn't listen to the restraining order. So, I packed up and left without warning. I tried to get as far away from him as possible. I thought Whispering Haven was far enough away. I hadn't heard a word from him since I left, and I cut off ties with anyone I thought might tell him where I was."

"So I'm guessing you didn't tell him where you'd gone," Carol surmised. Harriet shook her head.

"I don't know how he found out," she said. She fell silent as the waiter dropped off their drinks. Her hand shook as she picked up her glass, water sloshing down the side and spilling over her fingers. "But I recognized him in the photo you took. I got so scared that I ran."

"She called me almost right away," Eric said.

"How much do you know about it?" Carol asked.

His expression darkened. "I know enough," he said. There was something ominous about the way he said it, something that made the hairs on the back of her neck prickled. "The guy is bad news."

Carol sipped her drink, contemplating the declaration. "Why did you divorce him?" she asked. "I know it's personal, and normally I wouldn't ask. I'd just mind my own business. But if you're in trouble with the police, I can help. But only if I know everything."

Harriet drew her finger through the condensation on the table, creating spirals and swirls as she chewed the inside of her cheek. Carol waited, knowing that interjecting right now would only make things worse.

"I didn't know just how dangerous James was," Harriet muttered. "Not at first. When I first met him, he seemed sweet, charming. We were married for ten years. It wasn't until a couple of years into our marriage that he started changing. I don't know what happened. He just got mean, and I started getting scared." She took a deep breath. "And then I started hearing all these rumors about him."

"Rumors?"

Swallowing, as if afraid someone would overhear, she glanced around, looking at all the tables, lingering on the faces as though any one of the people might tell her story to the world if they overheard it. Eventually, she leaned in.

"That he was a conman, mostly," Harriet said. "That he'd been in jail, or close to it. He never went to prison while we were married. But once or twice I had these strange men show up at our house. Unsavory types, who kept dropping veiled threats. When I asked James about them, he'd wave them off and tell me not to worry. Eventually, it got to be too much, and I knew he was lying, even if I didn't know all the details."

"What happened after you broke up?"

"He started stalking me." She shivered, glancing at Eric before looking back down at the table and the water designs. "Kept showing up at my place, sent other people to talk to me and keep track of my comings and goings. I was terrified. Eventually, I got a restraining order. Not that that did much good. He just kept on harassing me."

"That's awful," Carol muttered. "I'm so sorry."

She rubbed her face, eyes filled with panic and pain as she tried to contain herself. "I really thought it would be different up here," she said. "I thought I could get away from it all."

"You have no idea how he found you?" Carol asked.

Harriet shook her head. "The only person I told about any of this is Eric," she said. "And any of my friends down south would know not to tell him anything if he came asking."

Carol tapped the side of her glass, contemplating the declaration. "Do you think it could have just been a coincidence?" she asked.

"I mean, anything's possible," Harriet said. At the same time, Eric shook his head.

"There's no way," he said. "He knew she was here. Someone told him."

"Who? And why?"

Eric shrugged, eyes dark. "Whoever did it, I don't think they were doing it to set up a happy reunion. If you ask me, someone's trying to frame her," he said. "It can't be a coincidence. He's murdered right after he rediscovers where his ex-wife lives?"

Carol didn't say anything for a long moment, studying Eric with interest. She could see the love and affection in his eyes, the fierce protectiveness.

"You're going to find out who did this, right?" Eric demanded.

"I'm going to do my best," Carol said. "That's all I can promise."

Eric's jaw twitched, but he nodded as though satisfied. Harriet let out an uneasy breath, leaning against Eric for support.

"Thank you, Carol," Harriet said. "You're a good friend."

As Carol looked at the couple, another question surfaced in her mind.

How far did Eric's loyalty go?

Would he kill for her?

Looking at the two of them, the way she leaned against him and the way he held her protectively, Carol knew without a doubt that, yes, he certainly would.

CHAPTER 6

Carol lounged on the couch, a purring Buttons curled on her stomach, when the doorbell rang. Moving the reluctant Buttons—who meowed in indignation as she was shifted from her comfortable slumber—she stood, stretched, and walked over, only to find Paul Morris lounging outside, a faint smile on his lips.

"Hey there," he said. "Was hoping I'd find you home."

"What's up?" Carol asked through a yawn.

"We got a lead on the murder weapon," Paul said.

Carol straightened, exhaustion forgotten as her heart jackhammered with excitement. "They found it? Where?"

"Not quite," he said. "But we've got somewhere to start. Ballistics are saying it was a Walther PDP. Fairly common pistol, in all honesty. But a guy named Derrick Redding reported his gun missing yesterday. Guess what type of gun it was?"

"I'm assuming a Walther PDP. Otherwise you wouldn't be calling me," she fired back.

He chuckled, the edges of his eyes crinkling. "Fair enough, and you're right," he said. "I was going to go have a little chat with him. I figured you might want to tag along."

"Now what on earth would give you that idea?" Carol retorted playfully. "Was it the insatiable curiosity, or the fact that we're technically partners?"

He bobbed his head from side to side. "A little of column A, a little of column B," he retorted. "So are you in?"

Except Carol was already closing and locking the door. "I'm offended you even had to ask," she said, slipping her key into her purse. "Now, are we going or are we going to stay here chatting?"

She followed Paul through the streets, the two of them chatting about nothing, neither bringing up the case yet, instead content to chat about the weather and local gossip. They both knew the conversation would eventually turn to the murder, but, for the moment, it was nice to focus on the other aspects of life.

Most of them, at least.

"So, I heard through the grapevine that Sarah Jean's birthday is coming up," he said, almost conversationally.

Carol groaned, rubbing her face. "Don't remind me," she muttered. "I've been stressing for a week about what to get her. She's impossible to shop for."

"I can believe it," he said. "Any ideas?"

DEADLY FLASH FROM THE PAST

"Maybe. I've been wondering if she could use some new gardening gear. Tools or gloves or something," Carol mused. She shook her head, brow furrowing in consternation. "No, no, that won't work. She always buys her own, and it's always state of the art. Last time I went over there, she had all new equipment. She's pretty serious about that type of thing."

Paul chortled. "Not going to lie, after everything you've done, I find it hard to believe that the thing tripping you up is a birthday gift."

"Presents were always Robert's strong suit," Carol grumbled.

"You'll figure it out." Paul patted her on the back as they pulled to a stop in front of a small colonial-style house. "Put those good detective skills to use. In the meantime, we've gotta talk to a man about a gun."

They marched up the path through the tidy, nondescript lawn. Carol couldn't help but think the entire array could have used some flowers. But before she could think further about it, they had reached the door.

The doorbell chime echoed, resonating through the house. A moment later, shadows moved behind the opaque windows. The door opened to reveal an average-looking man, his grey hair speckled with spots of lingering brown.

"Derrick Redding?" Paul asked.

"Yeah," he said, eyes darting between the two of them.

"We're private detectives," Paul said. "We wanted to check with you about your missing gun."

Derrick snorted, pushing the door further open. "Private detectives go after missing guns now, do they?" he grunted, his voice borderline derogatory.

Carol bristled, eyes narrowing. "They do when they might be involved in a murder," she retorted.

Derrick sobered immediately, his face going grim as his attention shifted from Paul to Carol and back again. "Is she serious?" he asked Paul.

"I can speak for myself," Carol retorted, eyes narrowing. "And yes, she is."

Derrick's jaw worked as he scrutinized the pair of them, seeming to debate whether or not he should comply.

"The police will be here soon enough," Paul promised, almost conversationally. "They'll probably be nicer to you if they find out you were cooperative with us."

"I don't have to talk to you," he groused.

"Sure you don't," Agreed an amicable Paul. "But you are going have to talk to the police. And we'll also be sure to let the police know how forthcoming you are with all your information next time my partner and I touch base with them."

The other man's eyes narrowed. He knew precisely what Paul was implying, and Paul didn't have any qualms with his thinly veiled threat. Her friend simply smiled warmly, as smooth a smile as any politician's.

A pause hung in the air, then Derrick sighed and stepped back.

"I didn't do anything," he said as he let them inside.

"We didn't say you did," Paul assured him. "We're just trying to figure out the timeline of things, and whether your gun might have had anything to do with it."

Derrick's house was small but tidy, filled with a mish-mash of décor and furniture that looked like he hadn't been able to decide between an 80s theme, a hunting lodge, or a modern take. The clash of styles assaulted Carol the instant she stepped inside.

"When was the guy—or girl, I guess—killed?" Derrick asked, closing the door behind him.

"Yesterday, we think," Paul said.

Derrick gave a *hah* of triumph. "In that case, there's no way it was me," he declared. "I reported my gun stolen two days ago. Police came and everything."

Carol tried not to let her frustration show—though she wasn't sure if that was because of his smugness, or that their best lead had just disappeared in a flash.

Glancing between them, Derrick folded his arms, back still stiff as if preparing himself for what he saw as an inevitable fight.

"Where do you normally keep your gun?" Paul asked.

"Lock box in the house. No idea how anyone got into it."

"Do you know a James Ratfield, Mr. Redding?" Carol asked, trying a different tactic.

He shrugged. "Never heard of him," he said. "Why? Is that the dead guy?"

"Spent any time in Georgia?" Paul asked instead of answering.

Derrick chuckled. "I mean, I've dipped through the airport a handful of times," he said. "But that's about it."

Unwilling to let this lead die without working every avenue, Carol held up the camera around her neck. She flicked through the photos still there, looking for a photo with a good shot of Ratfield. She found one and held her camera up to Derrick. "So you're saying you've never seen this man?" Carol asked.

Derrick squinted, then shook his head. "Nope. Never seen the guy in my life."

She tried not to show her disappointment too much, but that feeling of defeat still washed over her as she let the camera dangle from her neck.

"Is there anything else you can tell us?" Paul asked. "Either about the gun or something that may lead us to who stole it?"

Shooting Paul an incredulous look, he said, "Don't you think I would have told the cops if I had more information? I happen to want my gun back, and helping the police is the best way for that to happen."

Before Carol could fire back an ill-advised retort, Paul gave her a nudge, silently telling her to keep quiet.

"Thanks for meeting with us, Mr. Redding," Paul said. "I think that's all we've got at the moment."

Derrick nodded. "Well, if there's anything else you need,

you know where I am. And let me know if you find my gun, will you?"

"I'm sure you'll be one of the first people to know if it shows back up," Paul said.

"Good." Derrick nodded. "Because there are only a few reasons someone would steal a gun, and none of them are particularly pleasant."

With no other questions and no real way to proceed, Carol and Paul bid Derrick farewell before walking back outside empty-handed.

"Well, that was a dead end," Carol sighed as the door closed behind them. She blinked rapidly as the sun slammed into her eyes, the warmth of the day pushing down at her again after the cool interior of Derrick's home.

"Bit annoying," Paul agreed, craning his head upward to look at the beautiful, clear blue sky. "But that's the way it goes sometimes."

"What next?" she asked. "Go home?"

A sly smile spread across his face, eyes sparkling. "Not quite," he said, drawing out the word. "I've got another stop I want to check out."

Carol's eyes lit up. "Don't keep me in suspense!" she said.

"I say we go pay The Seaport Bed and Breakfast a little visit, don't you?" he asked.

CHAPTER 7

The Seaport Bed and Breakfast was a sprawling house surrounded by lush greenery and vibrant flowers. Carol slowed as they walked through the garden, eyes locked on the beautiful roses and peonies.

"I wonder if they get their plants from the local nursery or not," Carol mused as she began trailing behind Paul.

"You can ask them yourself." Paul chortled as he took Carol by the elbow and steered her to the front door.

"Can't I just take a couple of photos?" she pleaded.

"When we've finished," Paul said, only releasing her when they arrived at the large oak front door. "For now, let's focus on the task at hand."

Carol wanted to argue, but she bit her tongue, knowing he had a point even as her fingers itched to snap off photo after photo of the stunning foliage. She exhaled through her nose and forced her hands by her side, away from her camera.

He opened the door to reveal a grand foyer with cream-colored walls and elegant wooden floorboards. A large desk sat next to a carpeted staircase. A woman with shoulder-length, straight black hair looked up from the computer, her elegant face creasing into a smile.

"Good afternoon," she said. "Welcome to The Seaport Bed and Breakfast." She glanced between the two of them, a pleasant but neutral and unfamiliar smile on her face. "Are you two checking in?"

"We're not guests," Paul explained.

The woman nodded. "I was going to say. No suitcases. Are you meeting a friend here or?"

"We were actually hoping to talk to the owner," Paul said.

"You're in luck, then," the woman said. "You're speaking with her." She came around the desk and held out her hand. "I'm Petra."

"Paul Morris." He shook her hand. "And this is Carol Riddick."

"Those names sound vaguely familiar." Petra glanced between the two of them. "Are you two locals?"

"We are. So as much as I love this house and how cute it is, I'm afraid I'm not looking for a place to stay at the moment," Paul said.

"Though if any of my out-of-state relatives come through here, I'm going to point them here," Carol promised, eyes sweeping across the foyer.

Giving a small smile, Petra said, "That's very kind of you. Since you're not looking for a room, what can I do for you?"

DEADLY FLASH FROM THE PAST

"I wanted to ask you about a James Ratfield," Paul said.

Her face went strained, the friendliness in her expression icing over at the edges as the name. Something like anger flashed in her eyes. "I heard about that," she said. "What about him?"

"We're looking into his death on a consulting basis. We know he stayed here," Paul said. "I was hoping we could see his room."

"It won't do you any good," Petra said quickly—perhaps a little too quickly, Carol wondered. "The police have already come through here and taken everything."

Carol huffed. She should have guessed they were coming. If she hadn't been so startled by recognizing James Ratfield's body, she would have dragged Paul here the instant they'd left the dock, rather than hurried home to call Harriet.

"That's all right," Paul said mildly, still smiling. "Any chance we could take a look at his room, anyway? Also, I'd love to ask you a few questions, if you don't mind."

Petra tensed, and when she opened her mouth a moment later, Carol was certain she would say that, as a matter of fact, yes, she did mind, and would kick them out that instant. Based on the hesitation, she was almost certainly thinking it.

Instead, when she finally spoke, Petra said, "yes, of course. Let me get the key."

Pulling out a key from the drawer, she gave another charming smile and jerked her head, indicating they should follow her as she strolled up the stairs. As Petra guided them through the halls, Carol marveled at its size and the elegant décor.

"This place is gorgeous, by the way," Carol said.

Paul nodded, looking around with admiration. "I heard someone had renovated this old house," he said. "You've done an amazing job with it."

Petra beamed, pride and joy radiating off her. "Thank you so much," she said. "I worked really hard on it. I moved here a few months ago and just fell in love with the place. It took a lot, but I'm glad I kept with it."

Pulling up in front of a door, she inserted the key and opened the door, motioning for Carol and Paul to step inside.

The room was fairly simple, and it was obvious the police had gone through here already, and taken everything, including Ratfield's clothes.

"I told you there wasn't much to look at in here," she said.

"Still worth checking," Paul promised. "I appreciate you taking the time to talk."

"So what was it you wanted to ask me in particular?" Petra stood straight in the doorframe, arms folded.

"What day did he get in?" Paul asked.

"Three days ago," Petra said, with such speed that Carol and Paul exchanged surprised glances. The other woman gave a small, amused smile. "I had to check for the police when they asked me the same question."

"Anything strange about him?" Carol quizzed.

Petra shook her head, even as her lips turned into a frown. "Maybe? He kept to himself most of the time. Asked me once whether I knew of anywhere to get good food."

Carol tilted her head as she studied the other woman. Something about her posture, the way she seemed unwilling to look at either Carol or Paul for more than a couple of minutes, made her wonder if there was something else going on below the surface.

"Did you two have some sort of argument?" Carol asked.

Petra jumped, alarm flashing in her eyes before she managed to get control of herself. "No, of course not," she tittered. "What on earth would give you that idea?"

Carol shrugged, looking around the room again. "It's just a vibe," she admitted. "I get the impression he left a bad taste in your mouth."

Petra gave a high, false laugh so fake it would have been obvious to a deaf person. "What are you talking about? That's absolutely ridiculous."

Exchanging glances with Paul, an unspoken understanding rippled between the two of them. Her intuition about Petra had been right. She didn't like James Ratfield. The only question was why.

"It's fine if you didn't like him, you know," Paul said. "We already have evidence that he wasn't the nicest of people, and we already know he's had run-ins with other people in town."

Petra's laugh died, and she eyed the two of them uneasily, her shoulders stiff as if preparing for a fight.

"Anything you can tell us will help," Carol prodded, trying to be encouraging. "You not liking him isn't a crime. But we need as much information as possible to get to the bottom of it."

Petra pursed her lips, then nodded, albeit a little reluctantly. "He wasn't the nicest of people, to be completely honest," she finally admitted. "If you ask me, he was actually a bit of a scumbag. He kept trying to say there was something wrong with his room. He even tried to plant a dead mouse in the corner of the room to try to get a free stay. The only way I was able to prove it wasn't my fault is because I have a video of him coming inside with it."

"Seriously?" Carol's mouth dropped open.

"Honestly, I was going to ask him to leave if he hadn't died," Petra said. "I didn't want him trying anything else in my bed-and-breakfast."

"You think he would have, after you caught him the first time?" Paul asked.

"Absolutely."

"And why is that, exactly?" Paul tilted his head.

Petra hesitated, eyes darting from side to side, as if she'd been caught in a trap. A second later, that flash of what looked like panic vanished, the woman's features smoothing over as she shrugged.

"He just seemed the type," she said. "Like I said, real piece of work. I wouldn't have been surprised if he ended up trying to con me out of my entire bed-and-breakfast."

DEADLY FLASH FROM THE PAST

Despite trying to keep her face a mask, a spasm of intrigue rippled through Carol, breaching onto her face. Glancing at Paul, she could tell he was thinking along the same lines as her.

"He was a con man?" Carol asked. She already knew the answer from Harriet, but Petra seemed to know more than she was pretending to, and kept slipping up. If Carol could pierce through that lie, then maybe they could get another lead.

"He just seemed the type," Petra muttered, not looking at either Carol or Paul.

"Did he tell you why he was here?" Paul inquired.

"He said he was coming to patch things up with his ex-wife," Petra said. "Or something like that."

This time, instead of intrigue, it was alarm that jolted through Carol.

"Was his wife expecting him?" Carol asked.

Petra shrugged, tossing her hair back. "How should I know?" she asked. "I would assume so, though, if they were planning to reconcile." She glanced at her watch and added, with a clipped tone. "I appreciate you coming to visit and that you need answers, but I've got work to do, so I'm afraid I'm going to have to ask you to leave."

"What do you think?" Paul asked when they stepped outside.

"I think something is definitely wrong here," Carol said. "I don't know where Petra's getting her information from, but there's no way Harriet knew James was here until she saw him in that photo."

"You don't think she could have faked it? She might have lured him here." Paul pointed out. At Carol's glare, he held up his hands. "I have to ask. It's part of my job."

"She seemed genuinely horrified when she saw him in that photo," Carol mused. "I don't think you can fake that type of surprise."

Despite her firm assurances, a disquiet rippled through her. It wasn't looking good for Harriet. She needed to find the real killer, and fast.

Someone else has to have a motive, she thought. *I just have to figure out who.*

CHAPTER 8

"There's no way Harriet would do something like that." Sarah Jean shook her head. "Granted, I don't know her super well, but if you trust her, then that's good enough for me."

Sun streamed in through the window, Buttons claiming the best and brightest beam, that conveniently for her, and inconveniently for Carol, happened to be on the counter.

For the moment, however, Carol couldn't care less whether her cat had elected to ignore her 'don't get on the counter' rule. Her head continued to swim with concerns over Harriet and the problems there.

"I don't know," Carol admitted. "I mean, I've been fooled by people before. What if she's been lying to me this whole time?"

"I don't think that's possible," Sarah Jean declared. Her hand reached out to squeeze Carol's. "And even if she is, then you'll figure it out. I know you will. You're smarter than you give yourself credit for, and an excellent detective."

The shaky smile Carol returned was strained to say the least. If she was such a great detective, then she should have been able to figure out a gift for Sarah Jean by now. But none of the ideas she'd come up with over the last few days had made any sense. And she didn't want to ask Sarah Jean directly, because she worried it would make Carol seem inept.

All of this ran through her head. When she pulled herself back to reality, Sarah Jean stared expectantly at her.

"Sorry. Lost in thought." Carol blinked, forcing herself to focus. "What did you say?"

"I was saying that maybe you could find some hints about what's going on by looking through his past. I'm sure he's got a lot of skeletons in his closet. Surely a few of them are thirsty for blood and would be perfect suspects."

"You're not wrong." Carol straightened. "Maybe it was a crime of opportunity and had nothing to do with Harriet being here."

Something about that theory didn't sit right with her, however. It was all too much of a coincidence. There was no way that whoever killed Ratfield didn't also know about his ex-wife living in Whispering Haven.

"I still think it's best if you look into his past and see what you can come up with," encouraged Sarah Jean. "The more people you can find with motive, the less guilty Harriet will look."

DEADLY FLASH FROM THE PAST

Carol let out a tired sigh. Sarah Jean had a point, and it was as good a plan as any they had come up with so far.

"Harriet didn't give me many details," Carol muttered, rubbing her chin. "If she was telling the truth, then I think he kept her at arm's length for most of his work projects."

"I wonder if we can't look him up and find some interesting dirt," Sarah Jean mused, eyes sparkling with the potential for new gossip.

Pushing away from the table, she hurried over to the computer, Sarah Jean fast on her heels.

Typing away on the computer, Carol waited, barely breathing, as Sarah Jean peered over her shoulder.

It only took a couple of seconds for the search engine to load, and with it came a plethora of news articles relating to a James Ratfield of Atlanta, Georgia. None of them were particularly pleasant.

"This guy was a piece of work," Carol said, eyes darting across the computer screen. "He's been in jail a few times, though it looks like the last time was before he and Harriet got married."

"Con job after con job," Sarah Jean muttered, still hovering over Carol's shoulder as she read the gossip greedily. "A couple of assaults as well, it looks like. Wow, no wonder Harriet was so eager to get away from him."

"And no wonder why she was so afraid when she saw him," Carol added, mind going back to the day she had taken that fateful picture. It seemed so long ago, despite being less than forty-eight hours prior.

Thinking about the photos made her want to go through them again, hoping that maybe she would be able to find some clue she had missed the first time around. She was positive she could find the answer somewhere in there, if only she knew what to look for.

Pulling up the pictures again, she flipped through them, identifying every photo with James Ratfield in it and moving it to a separate folder. Seeing how many times James snuck into her photos sent a ripple of disquiet through her. How had she not noticed him before? And how long had he been tailing them? She shivered, trying to shake off the unease.

As she moved through the photos, her eyes snagged on something else in the background, something further away than James Ratfield.

Another figure.

He—she thought it was a he, at least—seemed to loom just out of focus, head down as if studying the ground or his shoes. A large hat covered their head and the top of their face, and bulky clothing—mildly out of season, given how warm it is—concealed most of his frame. Something about his presence instilled an air of disquiet and uncertainty as she studied the photo, a new chill washing over her. A new sneaking suspicion crossed her mind. She clicked to the next photo, only to have those suspicions confirmed. She nodded, jaw set as she found the exact same man lurking in the corner of another photo.

Again and again—each of the photos with James in the frame, the secondary figure hovered further back.

"Do you see that?" Carol asked.

DEADLY FLASH FROM THE PAST

"See what?"

Pointing to the unknown person, Carol said, "This one. They keep showing up."

"Who's that?" Sarah Jean asked, squinting as she leaned forward.

"That's what I want to figure out," Carol said, frowning. Was he about the same height as Eric? She couldn't tell. Something about the way the figure held themselves looked familiar, but she couldn't be positive. The hat and the clothes made it difficult to discern anything beyond broad generalities.

Which was probably the entire point, Carol thought, that uncomfortable chill crawling over her entire body.

Reading Carol's expression, a knowing smile spread across Sarah Jean's face. "I know that look," she declared. "You already have a theory, don't you?"

Swallowing, not looking away from the screen as she flitted through the photos, Carol admitted, "a little one, yes."

"Don't keep me in suspense!"

Carol hesitated; there was always the chance she was wrong. But if she couldn't trust Sarah Jean, she didn't know who she could. "I think they were following James," she said. "Not us."

Gasping, her friend's eyes widened as they turned back to the computer screen, a new interest glittering behind them.

"Our stalker had a stalker," she breathed with excitement. "Incredible."

Carol nodded, her own enthusiasm taking off now that her theory was out in the open. "If we find out who this is, we'll probably find someone who isn't Harriert who had a strong motive, and knew he was in town."

As Carol studied the photo, a new certainty crept over her. It also seemed now that Harriet's part in this story could no longer be a coincidence. Someone, the person following Ratfield in the photo, had known she was here and who she was.

Someone had used her as bait.

CHAPTER 9

Carol walked up the steps to the station, a bit of apprehension creeping upon her as she did. She needed to talk to Tex and tell him what she had learned, but the fear that she would accidentally find a way to implicate Harriet still lingered in the back of her head, a looming threat she was afraid might come to pass.

She pushed the fear from her mind. She was here to find a killer. If she did her job correctly, then Harriet would have nothing to worry about. She had to press forward.

She stepped into the bustling office, looking around, before walking up to the woman at the front desk.

"I was hoping I could talk to Tex," she said. The woman nodded, pushing back away from the desk and hurrying deeper into the station.

A few minutes later, the woman reemerged, Tex following behind her. He gave a warm smile and held out his hand. "Good to see you, Carol," he said. "Solve the case yet?"

"Not quite," Carol said. "But I've got some information for you that I think you might find interesting."

He tilted his head. "Well, I always like interesting information. Why don't you come back into my office?"

She followed Tex through the bullpen and deeper into the station, trying not to think about the last time she had been in Tex's office, where he had effectively accused her of murder. When they walked into the room, it didn't appear to have changed much. Messily tidy, the type of clutter that made sense to its owner though perhaps no one else. Several files lay spread across his desk, and a corkboard on the wall was covered with notes and flyers and a myriad of information.

"So, this interesting information." Tex leaned against his desk, watching her with polite interest.

"Did you know that James Ratfield was a con man?" Carol asked.

She had hoped that Tex's eyes would widen and that he would straighten up, perhaps the faintest trace of guilt on his face for assuming it was Harriet at the beginning. He would tell her how he was immediately going to pivot his investigation into looking at his old cons and thank her for bringing this vital information to his attention.

Instead, he nodded, no surprise anywhere on his face. Her hope sunk deep into her chest.

"I already heard all about that," Tex said. "He definitely wasn't up to much good. I spoke to a couple of officers in Atlanta. They said he wasn't surprised he wound up dead. The guy made a lot of enemies."

DEADLY FLASH FROM THE PAST

"That's part of my point," Carol said. "There are so many people who might have wanted him dead. Surely there are people other than Harriet who are a better fit for his murder."

He raised his hand, silencing her before she built up steam.

"Sure, there are other people who I would think are more likely to kill him based on his background," he admitted. "But the truth of the matter is, none of those people are up here. The only person in this area who knows James is Harriet. Therefore, she's the person with the best motive for his murder in Whispering Haven."

Carol clenched her jaw, trying not to scream. "Really, Tex, this is absurd," she argued. "She couldn't hurt a fly."

"She's your friend," Tex fired back. "You know that you're not impartial in this whole thing."

"I don't need to be impartial when I know she had an alibi," Carol pointed out. "Eric says she was with him all night."

He gave her an almost patronizing look. "Boyfriends don't typically make great alibis, Carol. Besides his word, there's nothing backing up her story, and there's every chance he's covering for her because he cares about her. Or maybe they did it together."

She decided not to bring up the fact that she'd had her suspicions about Eric as well. It wouldn't help out Harriet in the current situation. But the fact that Tex still refused to listen to her points grated at her, making her want to scream in frustration.

Trying to get a grip, she forced herself to remain calm as she brought up her next point. "What about him being here? How did he know Harriet was here?"

Something flickered across Tex's features for the first time, something a lot like doubt. "That's something we're still working on," he admitted. "We don't have a great answer for that one yet. Right now, the working theory is that Harriet told him herself, or got one of her friends to tell him to lure him up here. But we don't have any record of any conversations between them. We're still looking."

"You really think that Harriet would tell her dangerous ex where she was staying after a year of being away from him, solely so she could kill him when she was already out of his grasp?" Carol argued.

"There's a lot we still don't know," Tex said, more than a little annoyed, eyes flashing, a sign he was beginning to lose his patience. "Carol, I really appreciate you trying to help your friend, but if I'm going to let you and Paul stay on this case, you're going to need to show me you can be impartial. There's a chance your friend is guilty, and you have to accept that."

She's not, Carol thought, but didn't say. Instead, she responded, "I understand, Tex. I'm doing my best. I just want to point out any potential questions you haven't thought of yet. Devil's Advocate sort of thing."

"I'm sure," Tex drawled, his expression communicating he didn't believe her in the slightest.

"It's not her, Tex," she said.

"I know you don't think so," he said. "But I can't operate on your gut. I have to follow the evidence."

DEADLY FLASH FROM THE PAST

"In that case," Carol said, jutting out her chin. "I guess I'll just have to find you some more evidence."

Tex snorted, shaking his head as amusement crinkled his eyes. "I hope you do," he said. "I would love for you to prove me wrong."

The look in his eyes told her that he genuinely meant it.

"In the spirit of providing more avenues for you to explore and finding you some more evidence," Carol said, digging around in her purse. "I have some photos I think you might find interesting."

Tex raised his eyebrow, reaching out for the photos. He flicked through them, eyebrows rising toward his hairline with each photo.

"So that's James, of course," he said. "You weren't kidding when you said he was following you."

Carol nodded. "But..." she prompted eagerly, knowing he had noticed the same thing she had.

"But who is that person in the background?" he asked.

Carol bobbed her head up and down enthusiastically. "Exactly!" she said. "I noticed it when I was going through them. He's in every photo with James Ratfield in it, and none of the others."

"Hmm." He scanned the photo, then looked back up at Carol, one eyebrow raised. "I'm guessing you have a theory?" When she nodded, he spread his arms with in an inviting gesture, eyebrows raised, his lips quirking upward. "Don't keep me in suspense," he said.

"I think that someone was following James Ratfield," Carol said. "Which means that someone else in town knew he was here. Not only that, but whoever this was had a reason to follow James Ratfield. You don't do that if you were best friends in grade school."

"No, you don't." Tex didn't look convinced. He held up one of the photos, squinting as he scrutinized it. "I'm gonna need glasses before too long," he muttered to himself. "Anyway, Carol, this isn't definitive. It doesn't prove Harriet didn't have anything to do with any of it. All it proves is that Harriet knew James was in town before he died."

Carol's spirits plummeted as fast as a skydiver without a parachute. "So you're not going to look into it?" she asked.

Tex held up a hand again. "I'm not saying that," he lectured. "I'm just telling you that it doesn't get her off the hook, and there's no guarantee this person has anything to do with any of this. For all we know, he could just be a normal bystander walking home and happened to go the same direction as you."

She raised an incredulous eyebrow, and this time Tex actually chortled, holding up his hands in an almost placating gesture. "I know, I know," he said. "The odds there are pretty slim, but you have to admit there's a possibility."

"I'll admit it's a possibility as soon as you admit there's a chance that Harriet had nothing to do with any of this," she fired back.

"Fair enough. There's a chance Harriet has nothing to do with it," he said. His smile disappeared and he studied

Carol with a solemn intensity. "But the odds are slim on that one, Carol. I'm sorry. I know she's your friend, but the sooner you accept that she might be guilty, the sooner you can look at all the facts impartially.

CHAPTER 10

Carol angrily scratched off another two lines on the scrap sheet of paper, glowering at the words she'd struck through: birdhouse? New book (what authors does she like?).

Pushing away from the table, she muttered irritably to herself as she ran her fingers through her hair. Sarah Jean's birthday loomed closer every day, and she still couldn't figure out what to get her. Anxiety had begun to creep in, digging its claws into her.

Was she really this bad of a friend? Surely she knew Sarah Jean well enough to come up with *something*. So why did her brain remain stubbornly blank?

"Could she use something for the kitchen?" she asked herself. "Only I don't remember what she already has." She huffed, trying to remember the layout of Sarah Jean's kitchen and what was already there. The more she remembered, the more items she scratched off her mental list.

"Shoot," she grumbled, running her fingers through her hair. "This shouldn't be this hard."

Buttons hopped onto the table, stretching first one way, and then the other, before flopping down on the piece of paper. She blinked up slowly at Carol, then turned her attention to the pencil in front of her, eyes growing wide and whiskers extending as she batted at it, then swatted it off the table.

Carol laughed, eyes crinkling. "If that isn't a sign to stop, I don't know what is." She scratched Buttons behind the ears. She sighed as Buttons continued to purr. "I just wish she was easier to shop for. Or that Robert was here to do it for me. He'd come up with some out of the blue, random idea that would end up being absolutely perfect. Best I can come up with right now is a dinner on me, which isn't exactly special, now is it?"

Buttons purred, opening and closing her eyes as she looked at her human affectionately.

"At least she isn't having a birthday party," Carol said, scratching Buttons beneath the chin. "Otherwise I don't know what I would do." She sighed. "I think I'm going crazy. I'm spinning in circles."

Forcing herself to take a break from thinking about presents, her mind went to Harriet again, and she worried her lip. She still needed to find someone with motive that wasn't Harriet. She felt as though she had only scratched the surface during her last foray into research.

"Well at least I'll be productive while I'm procrastinating," Carol muttered, walking to the computer.

DEADLY FLASH FROM THE PAST

The first search she did was actually for Harriet and James. She found the police records that showed she had filed for a restraining order, and also notes that he had ignored the order twice, the second time only a handful of days before she had probably moved from Atlanta. She found the short police reports for both of those, but nothing that really provided her any useful information beyond confirming Harriet's story, nothing that would exonerate her.

"I need to look more into his past," she muttered. That's where the key would be; she was certain of it.

She typed in his name alone, and her eyebrows shot up. There was a James Ratfield. Except this James Ratfield wasn't located in Atlanta. All the articles around him came from Illinois, not far from Chicago. Raising her eyebrows, she started reading.

It was definitely the same James Ratfield. The photo associated with the articles was all the man she had seen dead at the harbor just a couple of days ago, the same man who had stalked Harriet through the town. Several years younger, somewhere in his twenties, but certainly the same man.

He'd been handsome, too. Firm jaw, dark, swooping hair and piercing eyes. He seemed like the quintessential con man, the type of person that people immediately trusted and liked, even through the red flags. That thought alone was enough to make her bristle. And as she continued digging through his past, her rage and incredulity only grew.

A couple of police reports, one where he had a short stint in jail, and another that had been knocked down to parole, both of which had to do with conning people out of their money. Granted, any of these could be worthy of someone hating him. However, when she pulled up information on the victims mentioned in the report, all of those showed them living hundreds of miles away from Whispering Haven. Besides, the cons mentioned didn't seem horrible enough to warrant James' murder, even if they proved he was a horrible human being.

Her hopes of exonerating Harriet began diminishing more and more by the minute. Her stomach churned as her heart ached with dread. Then, she clicked on an article, and the breath rushed out of her throat.

> James Ratfield, 30, has been found not-guilty due to a mistrial of the manslaughter of Alexandra Gibson, 28. The judge threw out the case due to the mishandling of evidence. During the announcement, the judge admonished the prosecution for their sloppy behavior, stating that he 'had never seen such an egregious blunder' on the part of the prosecution. While the defense's lawyer applauded the decision, saying that 'justice persevered' today, several jurors, on the condition of anonymity, stated that they would certainly have found him guilty had there not been a mistrial. "The evidence was overwhelming," one of them said. "Pity that the guy gets to walk free."

She sucked in a breath, reading and rereading the article, trying to absorb the information even as it seemed impossible. She could barely believe her eyes. Hurriedly, she typed in "Alexandra Gibson," revealing a handful of new articles detailing the incident. It appeared that, allegedly, Ratfield had sold Alexandra a car, only for it to stall a couple of days later in the middle of the highway, resulting in a collision that had left one injured and Alexandra dead.

Her brow furrowed. It definitely seemed as though the accident had taken place before he had met Harriet. Based on the articles, it seemed rather obvious that poor Alexandra had died due to one of Ratfield's schemes going wrong. A bad con job that had resulted in someone's death and him moving to Atlanta to go underground.

Pulling up a photo revealed a pretty young woman with mousy brown hair and freckles along the bridge of her nose. Her wide smile made her eyes sparkle. She was in the prime of her life; the photo showing a woman full of hope and optimism for the future.

And James Ratfield had snuffed out her life.

The thought made her fingers tighten around the computer mouse, wondering how she would feel if this had happened to one of her nieces. Furious, certainly. There's no telling what she would do.

Studying Alexandra's photo, she couldn't deny there was something familiar about the woman, somewhere around the eyes and lips. She squinted, trying to determine what might have triggered her memory and coming up blank.

Still, despite the obvious tragedy, she couldn't find anything connecting Alexandra or her family to Whispering Haven or Ratfield's death.

She kept going through, trying to dig up anything else, looking for more leads. She found one more article, and this one pulled her up short, shocking her almost as much as the one about Alexandra Gibson.

> The family of Arrya Bedi is suing James Ratfield, claiming that he manipulated the wealthy dowager into changing her will to bequeath most of her money to him.
>
> Ratfield, for his part, claims that Bedi bequeathed the money to him out of gratitude for helping her out. He and his lawyers also point out that the family was still left with significant funds, including the house, her art collection, among other items.
>
> The Bedis' lawyer states that, regardless of what Arrya left her family, that doesn't change the fact that Ratfield conned the woman for his own advantage. He says that he's confident that justice will prove Ratfield has no rightful claim to the funds.

Despite the unnamed lawyer's optimism, another article proved that their attempts to reclaim the wealth had been unsuccessful. Ratfield had gotten away with another con.

Bedi...the name rang a bell. Her brow furrowed as she tried to recall where she had heard that name recently. Then her eyes flew open wide as the name finally struck home.

Bedi. Petra Bedi. The owner of the B&B where James Ratfield had stayed.

Hurriedly, barely breathing, Carol typed furiously, looking up Petra Bedi to see if she was connected to the wealthy Arrya. If she was in anyway related, then Petra not only knew who James Ratfield was, but she would have significant motive to want him dead.

At first, she couldn't find a connection, and she began to wonder if it might just be a wild coincidence. She huffed, head spinning as her mind reeled.

She was just about to give up when she struck gold. Arrya Bedi's obituary, set a few months before the scandalous article, listed a Petra Bedi as the deceased's granddaughter.

Staring, hope blossomed in her chest as the implication of the discovery hit her full-force.

Someone else had known James Ratfield was in town, and had more than enough reason to kill him.

CHAPTER 11

Sarah Jean sat cross-legged on the couch, sipping her tea as Buttons curled into a ball next to her, purring whenever Sarah Jean scratched her with perfect nails.

"You know, I could really use some new pruning sheers," Carol said casually, eyeing Sarah Jean's reaction. "How are yours?"

Sarah Jean's eyes lit up and she straightened with excitement. "You know, I just got a new pair last week! I absolutely adore them. I think Jim over at the hardware store still has some of them tucked away somewhere, if you went to look for it."

Carol tried to bite back a hiss of frustration. "What about the rest of your gardening gear?" she asked. "How is that holding up?"

"Just fine! I actually went out and bought a whole new set a few weeks ago, and got my favorite trowel sharpened. Everything is spic and span."

Exactly as Carol had feared and suspected. Her friend was the type of person who took care of things herself and didn't wait for others.

Trying a different tactic, she inquired, "Picked up any new hobbies lately?"

"Gardening, work, and gossip are taking up all of my time at the moment." Sarah Jean winked. "Though I might try yoga at some point."

Fantastic! Maybe I could get her a yoga mat.

"After all, I already have the mat for it."

Carol's brief glimmer of hope sank faster than the Titanic. She sipped at her coffee, trying to hide the grimace of frustration. She loved Sarah Jean to pieces, and she wanted to do something nice for her friend. That seemed more impossible by the second.

For a brief moment, she considered simply asking Sarah Jean what she wanted for her birthday. Except her sense of pride seemed incapable of allowing her to let the words pass her lips. She wanted her gifts to be a surprise, not something the recipient expected. It felt more meaningful to her, more impactful, if you could pull that off.

That didn't stop the fact that she was beginning to grow very tempted by the prospect. She would rather have a gift on time than a belated one. But she still had a few days. Maybe she could figure out something before then. She'd leave asking to a last-ditch, worst-case scenario. In the meantime, she would keep prodding.

Before she could poke further, however, Sarah Jean changed the subject.

DEADLY FLASH FROM THE PAST

"How is the case going?" she inquired. "Do you have any exciting pieces of information?"

"A bit," Carol hedged, debating just how much to tell Sarah Jean. She knew her friend wouldn't intentionally spill gossip all over town, but if she got overexcited—and based on the way this case was going, that was certainly a possibility—then any information Carol told her would be widely known by the end of the day.

At the same time, however, it was her friend, and she couldn't keep her in the dark, not when it would all come spilling out eventually, anyway.

"Did you find out who our mystery man is?" Sarah Jean asked, straightening as her eyes glittered with excitement.

She shook her head, much to Sarak Jean's annoyance. "I've been trying to figure out if there are any connections to James Ratfield that don't involve Harriet," she explained.

That re-engaged her friend. She straightened again. "Anything interesting?"

"I want to talk to Petra, actually," Carol said, explaining what she had uncovered online. Sarah Jean's eyes grew wide as saucers at the revelation.

"Really?" Sarah Jean gasped. When Carol nodded, she shot to her feet. "Then what on earth are we doing sitting here? We should be going and having a lovely little chat with Petra and get some more information, don't you think?"

As they walked through the center of town, Carol's mind wandered far away from Petra and back to the problem of Sarah Jean. She kept running ideas through her mind, testing out possibilities as the two of them walked.

They walked past a nursery, with lush plants in full bloom spilling out of their pots with life. Her eyes scanned the other additions, wondering if maybe she could use the opportunity to prod more.

"Wouldn't something like that be fun to have?" Carol asked, pointing to a charming stone birdbath with a snoozing cat carved at its base. "It's so cute."

"It's darling," Sarah Jean said. "You know, it's quite similar to one I ordered just last week."

There goes another one, Carol thought bitterly.

Carol pointed into a couple of windows as they strolled past, pointing at a cute jacket in one and some cute pottery in another. Sarah Jean responded to each how she had something just like it at home.

By the time they reached the bed-and-breakfast, Carol was as close to coming up with a birthday gift idea as Australia was to Canada.

Petra smiled when the two of them walked into the house. Her smile faltered, however, when she realized that one of her guests was Carol.

"Can I help you?" she asked.

"Actually, yes." Carol wished she had thought to find a photo of Arrya Bedi, just to confirm her belief. If she'd been able to prove there were physical similarities, her accusation would come across as a lot more believable.

Petra nodded, still beaming, completely oblivious of the storm about to come her way. "Are you looking for a room?" she asked. "Maybe for one of your relatives? Who's coming into town? Or maybe you're looking for a staycation?"

"Not quite," Sarah Jean said, staring Petra down with a look so severe that a full-grown man would have withered beneath it. Petra's own smile faltered, glancing between the two women, eyes lingering on Carol as she searched for an explanation.

"Why didn't you tell me you knew James Ratfield?" Carol demanded.

Petra's eyes flashed with alarm. Then she gave a shrill laugh, though it didn't reach her eyes.

"You're joking, right?" she asked. "You can't be serious."

"Really?" Carol raised an eyebrow. "So he didn't steal a bunch of money from your grandmother by convincing her to change her will?"

The forced smile on Petra's face died.

"What are you talking about?" she asked, though not particularly convincing.

"I really should have printed out the article," Carol muttered to Sarah Jean, before turning back to Petra. "I did my research. I know she was your grandmother. I can't imagine how frustrating it must have been to have all that money snatched from you like that."

Petra hesitated, looking around. Finally, she sighed, shoulders sagging. "It was infuriating," she admitted. "Not because of the money. Grandmother was old and her memory was terrible. He took advantage of her, and that's what angered me. If he had actually cared about her and she had given him the money, I wouldn't have batted an eye—we got the house and her art collection was worth millions. We didn't need more money." Her eyes darkened, anger flashing across her face. "But he didn't care about her at all/ He just wanted her money. When Mom tried to call him out on it all those years ago, he said it didn't matter. He claimed—" she took a deep breath, fists curling as she tried to contain her anger. "He claimed that it didn't matter, because he still made her happy in the end."

"What happened when you saw him?" Carol asked. "And surely you recognized the name when he signed in."

Petra shook her head. "When he booked, he used a fake name. I didn't make the connection at first, even though I thought he looked familiar. It wasn't until he brought the rat in that I realized who he was. I mean, it wasn't as though I had much interaction with him when it all happened. My parents kept me away from most of it, except for when I legally had to be there."

"He didn't recognize you?" Carol asked. "After your family sued him? Surely he wouldn't have stayed here if he'd recognized you."

She laughed. "He was so full of himself that he probably had forgotten all about us," she said. "Plus, I was—what, ten or so? It's not as though he would have connected a little kid to me."

"And why didn't you kick him out when you did recognize him?" Sarah Jean asked.

"I was so surprised I wasn't sure I was right," Petra admitted. "Like I said, I was a kid. I haven't even thought of him in years."

"How did you feel when you did find out?" Carol asked.

Petra's eyes narrowed, her jaw twitching as she stared at Carol with suspicion. "I don't like all these questions," she said. "I've tolerated them up until now because you caught me off guard. But I don't like your implications. You're not the police, and I don't have to talk to you."

"We're trying to help a friend," Carol began, though Petra interrupted her.

"By implicating me?" she demanded. "I appreciate the loyalty to your friend, but I'm not about to be your patsy."

"That's not—"

"Thank you for coming in," Petra said, eyes flashing. "But I'm afraid I'm going to have to ask you to leave."

CHAPTER 12

Harriet cracked the door open. A flash of relief sparked in the one visible eye, then she opened the door fully.

"Hi, Carol," she said. "Sorry about that. Come on in."

"Worried about the police?" Carol asked as she stepped into the foyer.

Harriet shook her head, hands trembling slightly as she closed the door. "Police are fine—well, as fine as they can be at the moment. But I've had a few nosy people poking around," she explained.

"Fiona?" Carol asked, raising an eyebrow.

"Among others. Actually, Fiona wasn't too bad. She was obviously snooping for gossip, but she seemed genuinely concerned at the same time. A few of the others..." she trailed off, a faraway look in her eye, but she shook her head, forcing a smile on her face."

"The police let you go," she reminded Harriet. "They didn't have enough information to arrest you." She didn't add the word *yet*. "Otherwise you'd be in a cell right now."

"No. But they did make it quite obvious that I was suspect number one." Harriet heaved a sigh as they walked into the living room, where Eric sat reading a book. He glanced up when they entered, and slammed the book shut, tossing it without bothering to mark his spot.

"Hey, Carol," he said. "Any word yet?" The hope in his face made her stomach ache with guilt. She wanted more than anything to give these two good news. Instead, the best she could provide was neutral.

"I've got a couple of leads," Carol admitted, trying not to raise their hopes too much. "But right now, they're sort of loose threads that have the potential to become something more. I was actually hoping that I could get a bit more information from the two of you, something that might either help absolve you, or shed some light on another suspect."

"Of course." Eric bobbed his head up and down. "Anything."

"First things first." Carol dipped her hand into her purse, withdrawing a cluster of photos from its depths. "I was hoping you could identify the man in these photos."

Harriet didn't take the photos at first. Her brow furrowed in confusion. "We know who it is," she said. "It's James."

"Not that person. The one further back."

Her forehead creasing even further, Harriet took the photos. She studied each of them, holding them close to her

DEADLY FLASH FROM THE PAST

face, searching for any detail that might give her a clue as to the man's identity. Carol held her breath, hoping against hope this might lead to something.

Then Harriet shook her head, and Carol exhaled in disappointment.

As Harriet passed the photos to Eric, she asked, "I'm sorry. I've never seen them before." At Carol's disappointed reaction, she asked. "Should I have?"

"It would have helped," Carol admitted. "But it's not your fault. What about you, Eric?"

But Eric was already shaking his head. "Sorry." He handed back the photos. "How important is finding the guy? I can pass the pictures around, but he's so far away I'm not sure it would do much good."

"It looks like he's trying to hide his face," Harriet mused.

"I was hoping you might recognize him from James' past," Carol said.

"He didn't talk much about it," Harrier admitted. "I'd always ask, and he would find a way to change the subject in a way that I wouldn't realize what he was doing until after the conversation had finished."

"I'll keep looking for him," Carol promised, tucking the photos away. "What were the two of you doing that night, anyway?"

"Honestly? Just watching a movie." Harriet shivered. "After I saw James in the photo, I called Eric and told him what happened. He was so sweet. He dropped everything he was doing at work to come home and make sure I was okay. He suggested we turn on a movie, so we pulled up my favorite —*The Princess Bride*—and he made the two of us popcorn and we just stayed home the whole evening."

"And you told Tex this?"

Harriet's smile faltered. "Yes. He said it was easy enough to just turn on a movie and leave it playing while we left to go take care of James."

Huffing, Carol ran her fingers through her hair, glaring at the floor. The problem was that Tex had a point. It was a shoddy alibi, one with so many holes in it that it would have made Swiss cheese envious. It wasn't going to help Harriet in the slightest. No, the only thing that would fully exonerate Harriet was finding the real killer, and she had a funny feeling that time was running out.

"I did some research into him a bit," Carol said. "You two met in Atlanta, right?" When Harriet nodded, she asked, "What did he tell you about his life before the two of you met?"

Harriet's brow furrowed. "Not much," she said. "He said he had done some real estate and construction, and that he'd had some bad experiences there, so had moved to different businesses. Like I said, he seemed to have his hand in everything." She laughed. "That really should have been a clue for me to run in the other direction. He was always so cagey. But he was so charming that I never realized what lurked below the surface until it was too late."

Carol nodded. "Was he wealthy?" she asked.

Harriet blinked in confusion. "Yes, actually," she said. "He got an inheritance from his grandmother. Though if you were to talk to him, he would act like he barely had a dime to his name. He hated paying for anything when he could get someone else to do it. How did you know?"

Carol chewed the inside of her cheek. "Have you ever heard of the Bedi family?" When Harriet shook her head, she gave her a brief summation of the information she'd uncovered and her conversation with Petra. The longer she spoke, the paler Harriet's face turned.

"That's terrible," Harriet muttered. She sighed, pulling her knees into her chest like a little kid as she sat on the couch. "You know he left me more or less penniless when we divorced. He managed to get an incredible lawyer."

Eric grumbled, eyes flashing with rage. "The guy was a complete scumbag," he growled. His features softened as he looked at Harriet, his hand going to her back. "But she managed to build herself back up despite him."

Smiling up at him, Harriet leaned into the touch.

Carol bit her tongue. She knew she had to ask this next bit, but she wasn't sure how.

She shook her head, forcing her nerves to scatter. She had to ask.

"Do you know anything about an Alexandra Gibson?" Carol asked.

Harriet blinked, tilting her head. "No. I'm sorry. Should I?"

"I'm not sure," Carol said. "Probably not, based on how much he told you about his past. Apparently, he sold her a lemon car, and it broke down on the highway, resulting in a crash. She died, and the family tried to sue James, only he managed to get off."

Harriet's face had grown waxen and pale, growing more so with every word. She sank onto the couch, eyes far away.

"No," she said, her voice hoarse. "No. I never heard anything about that." She hesitated, glancing back up at Carol. "Is there a chance he didn't do it?" she asked, a hint of desperation in her voice. "I know he was dangerous and an awful person, but murder..." she trailed off, shaking her head as she tried to reconcile the man she once loved with this new information.

Eric sat next to her, wrapping his arm around her.

"I'm sorry," he said. "But it's probably true. After all, I doubt he was coming up here to give you back your old photos."

The words and implication sent a chill through Carol as she knew the truth behind them. James didn't come here with good intentions. Meeting Eric's eyes, she knew he had understood this from the beginning. Again, that question floated in her mind: how far would he go to protect her?

CHAPTER 13

Carol browsed the aisles, brow furrowed as she hummed to herself. Her focus flipped between the case and the task at hand, which happened to be finding a gift for Sarah Jean.

She had tried the bookshop in town, though it was mostly cluttered with tourist books, and the only potentially interesting book had been a gardening book twenty years out of date, rendering it almost useless.

She was running out of ideas and running out of time. As such, she was beginning to get desperate. She'd been desperate before, but now she could practically see the clock ticking down in front of her eyes, and here the infuriating tick-tock as it counted down.

Which was how she had found herself in a cute store with all sorts of art and souvenirs. Everything from elegant landscapes to kitschy ceramic kittens, their paws raised in the air as they looked back at you with identical adorable expressions. None of them screamed Sarah Jean, but some of them could suit. She could see her liking the stained glass bird currently hanging on the wall, or the windchimes with glass beads dangling from the end.

"Can I help you?" a vaguely familiar voice asked.

"Yes, actually," Carol said. She began to turn. "I'm looking for—"

She cut herself off in shock when she saw the square face looking down at her. The man blinked in shock, taking his own step back as the two of them regarded one another. It was Derrick Redding, the man whose gun might have been used in the murder.

He seemed, however, to have already recognized her. He'd folded his arms in front of his chest, eyebrow raised, lips thin and unsmiling.

Out of everything that could have happened, this wasn't one of them. She didn't like the way he glared at her, a cloud of distrust swirling around him. The last thing she wanted was for him to think she was here to interrogate him.

"Oh, hello," Carol said, smiling. She furrowed her brow as she pretended to only vaguely remember him. "Derrick, right? Sorry, I'm terrible with names."

"It's all right," he said, some of the tension in him ebbing. He arched an eyebrow, tilting his head. "Are you here to ask me more questions?" A layer of jovial friendliness overlay the words, but something about the way he asked made her skin prickle.

The truth was, she might as well try to get more information out of him, now that she was here. But the best way for her to do that would be to go about it in a more subtle way.

"I'm looking for a gift for my friend," Carol said. "I've been struggling to figure out something."

Derrick nodded, the hints of suspicion ebbing from his expression. He glanced around, scratching his chin.

"Not normally the type of place you go looking for gifts," he mused. "At least not for friends."

"You're telling me," Carol sighed. "At this point, though, I'm desperate."

He chuckled. "Does she like art?" he asked.

"Um..." she paused, hesitating. "I think so."

He raised an eyebrow, the edges of his lips tilting upward. "I see," he said. "Well, I'm sure we've got something here for her. I like to say that my shop has something for everyone."

"You own this place?" Carol glanced around. Suddenly, the eclectic way he designed his house made more sense.

He nodded. "Bought it a few years ago," he said. "I'd always dreamed about having a shop. Figured I should just go ahead and do it instead of just talking about it all the time, you know?"

"Well, it's paid off," she said.

He grinned. "Glad you approve," he said. He jerked his head. "Let's see if we can find something for your friend. Who is it?"

"Sarah Jean."

He chortled, eyes sparkling. "Yeah, she sure is something. I can believe you'd have some trouble finding something for her."

"You know her?" Carol asked, nothing bothering to hide her surprise.

He shrugged, continuing to lead her through the shop, pointing to various items. "I know most people in the area," he explained. "I like to think I've got my finger on the pulse of the town."

"How long have you lived here?" She tittered. "I've been here for a year and I still get spun around some of the time. My memory isn't what it used to be, you know."

"I've been here for a while," he said.

Carol snapped her fingers. "That's right. You know, after we met, I suddenly realized why the name sounded so familiar. You're a staple in Whispering Haven! Everyone seems to know you. They all say you're a real handyman and always first to help volunteer for something."

Derrick grinned, straightening a bit at the praise. "I like to think that's the case," he said. "But that's the sort of thing you do when you've lived in a small town for some time. Whispering Haven has been good for me. I wanted to be able to give something back."

"Well, that's very sweet of you." Carol patted his arm. "Not everyone would do that. What brought you here in the first place? Relatives?"

His smile faltered. "No, nothing like that," he said. "I wanted to get away from things. My fiancé died, and I wanted to get away from all the drama. Whispering Haven seemed like the perfect place to reset."

The pain on his face was genuine. He coughed, looking away from Carol. Her heart broke. You couldn't fake that type of pain; she knew from experience.

"My husband died a little over a year ago," she said. "I moved all the way from Phoenix to get away from it all. I know a bit about what that's like. I keep hoping it'll get better...and it has...but maybe not as quickly as I would have liked."

Derrick nodded, face still contorted with grief. "It does get easier," he said. "Sometimes. Other times, not so much. You'd think fifteen years would help...sometimes it still feels like it was yesterday." He chortled, shaking his head. "Sorry. That's probably not the type of thing you want to hear."

"It's what I would expect." She took a deep breath. "I'll miss him every day. But that's part of getting older. You start to understand that death really is a part of life."

He nodded, but he still looked tired and worn down. "It's definitely hard." He shook his head to clear it, pulling on a customer service smile. "But, hey, that's how it goes sometimes. Do you think she would like this?"

They wandered through, but, as seemed to be the case everywhere, nothing caught Carol's eye. As they finished the tour of the shop, she shook her head. "Sorry, but thanks for your time. It was worth a shot."

"All good." He shrugged. "Happy to help."

"By the way, did the police ever find your gun?" It was the

first time she had really properly brought up the case. She watched his reaction to gauge his response.

He shook his head. "If they have, they haven't told me," he grumbled. "Shame. I was really hoping to go to the range this coming weekend."

"You said you keep the gun in a gun safe, right?" she asked. He nodded. "Who knew about the pistol?"

He shrugged. "Anyone who saw me at the range, I suppose?"

"What about the gun safe? Anyone who knew the combination?"

Another shrug. "Someone must have guessed it," he said.

Carol's brow furrowed. "So, you're saying someone broke in, stole the gun in your locked safe, then left without touching anything?"

Derrick shrugged. "There's a chance I left the safe unlocked by mistake. Someone broke in looking for anything, saw it unlocked. Crime of opportunity."

"You don't feel like that's too many coincidences?" Carol asked.

Something flickered across Derrick's expression. "I don't know what you're talking about," he said.

"It just feels a little off, that's all," Carol said.

Derrick hesitated, then sighed. He glowered at her. "Okay, so maybe I was lying," he grumbled. "Maybe it wasn't at home. Maybe it was at the shooting range, and I didn't want to let the police know that I had been that irresponsible with my gun. I looked away from it for two seconds and bam! I figured it might be easier and less hassle for me if I said it got stolen from my house."

"You should probably tell the police that," Carol said. "Otherwise they're going to look in the wrong place for a killer."

"What difference does it make where I was?" he asked, shrugging. "The point was it was stolen."

Carol wanted to argue, to point out that it made a significant difference. But before she could get out a word, Derrick's attention slid off her, glancing toward the door as a tourist couple wandered in.

"I think we're done here," he said. "Thanks for looking. If you want something for your friend, you know where to find me."

"Of course."

He hesitated, glancing to the newcomers, before leaning over and whispering, "If you would keep the gun bit between us, I'll give you a discount."

He strolled away, leaving Carol standing in the middle of his store, staring after him as even more questions than before swirled in her head.

CHAPTER 14

As Carol jerked out some of the weeds, contemplating everything that had happened and how much more they had to do, how many more questions they had to answer, the phone rang.

"Hey, got something you might find interesting," Paul said by way of greeting the instant she answered. "What's the fastest you can get down to my office?"

"If I speed? Five. If I try to avoid the ire of the police, then ten. So we'll say five."

A chuckle echoed over the phone. "Let's try not to annoy the police too much right now. Ten minutes is more than fine."

She hung up, looking at Buttons who lounged in a sunny patch of grass, watching Carol with bright, intelligent eyes.

"Sorry, but it's time to hurry back inside," Carol said.

As if she could understand, Buttons yawned, got to her feet, stretched, and then promptly turned her back to Carol and plopped right back down in the grass, grooming herself.

"Very cute." Carol plucked the cat from the ground, earning her an irritated flick of the ear as she carried the cat back inside.

Paul's office was a cramped room, made even smaller by the clutter that seemed to swallow the entirety of the space. The desk, a little too large for the room, sat so close to the filing cabinet that the drawers banged into its side, scuffing the corner. The walls were plastered with papers about cases, missing persons, and all sorts of other things.

Paul scooted out from behind his desk when Carol pushed open the unlocked door.

"You need a cleaner," Carol teased by way of greeting, her go-to response whenever she had to step foot inside the office.

"I'll have you know I cleaned yesterday," he said. "This is all brand new."

He turned to walk back into the center of the office before turning back to face Carol, waiting for her to broach the subject.

"What've you got?" Carol asked. "You dragged me away from my rose bush, so it better be important."

Paul grinned broadly. "So, the police still haven't been able to get access to James' emails."

"That doesn't seem like something to be happy about," Carol said, frowning as she studied her partner's expression. "And definitely not worth dragging me away from my garden."

Paul kept grinning. "That's because I don't always rely on the police's computer skills," he quipped. "I know people who work a lot, lot faster than the police. The benefits of not having to worry about bureaucracy. Though maybe don't tell Tex that. I don't know how kindly he'll take to knowing that we may have bent a couple of rules to beat him to the punch."

"If he asks, I'll tell him that you figured it out on your own," Carol said, practically bouncing on the balls of her feet as she waited to hear what he had discovered. "Now tell me before I have a stroke out of excitement. I'm not getting any younger, you know."

"We found an email, actually," Paul said, sobering a little. "It was in his deleted trash, to be more accurate. My contacts know their way around the internet to be able to pull that up. Nowadays, nothing is permanently deleted."

Carol glowered, and Paul's grin grew wider, confirming her suspicion that he was dragging this out for the fun of it.

"Tell me what you found out, or Tex might have another murder to solve," she threatened with no real malice, earning a chuckle from Paul.

"All right, all right." He held up his hands in concession even as his eyes sparkled with mirth. "Are you sure you don't want lunch first? We can—"

"Paul!"

"Okay, fair enough." He took a deep breath. "The recovered email talked about Harriet. It came from what looks to be an anonymous source, unfortunately."

"What did it say?"

"It said that James might be interested to know that Harriet currently resides in Whispering Haven," he said. He paused, before adding, "It also had a link to the Seaport B&B."

Carol gaped. "Really?" she asked.

Paul nodded, his expression turning grim. "James sent back an email asking for proof. Less than ten minutes later came a photo of Harriet out by the ocean. James said thanks and that was the end of it."

"Anything else?" Carol asked. "Bookings or anything?"

Paul shook his head. "None that we could find on that particular email," he admitted. "But, I'm not surprised. Petra told us he booked under a false name. That wouldn't be particularly useful to him if he used his normal email. My bet is that he's got a bunch of different identities and an email for each of them. Based on our guess of what he was planning on doing up here, I think he was doing his best to cover his tracks."

He walked out, squeezing behind his desk. The filing cabinet thumped softly against the desk as he opened it, pulling out a manilla envelope. Without ceremony, he turned and held it out to Carol.

Flipping it open, she could see it was exactly what Paul had told her it was. She drank it in greedily, eyes scanning the page while Paul watched. Finally, she glanced up.

"When are we going to tell Tex about all this?" she asked.

"I was thinking right about now," he retorted, raising an eyebrow. "Do you want to drive or should I?"

Tex glanced up the moment Paul and Carol strolled into his office, one eyebrow raised as he leaned back in his chair. He tapped his pencil on the side of his thigh.

"Jenny said you told her you've got something important?" he asked, referring to the secretary who had just walked them back.

"I like to think I only ever bother you when it's something important," Paul retorted.

"Yeah? What about that time you went fishing when I couldn't join, and you pestered me about the giant fish you caught for a week?"

"That was bragging. Entirely different. Besides, I can't help it if you were too busy to take time off and missed some massive bass."

Tex raised an eyebrow. "You gonna tell me what you apparently found, or did you come just to brag?" he asked without a real hint of annoyance."

"Anyway," Paul said. "I was able to get into James' email through perfectly legal and not-questionable-at-all means, and I found something we thought you might like."

"Broke into it about an hour ago, actually," Tex said.

"You find the deleted emails?" Paul asked.

Tex straightened, fully on alert for the first time since Carol and Paul had strolled into his office.

"Deleted emails as in the trash, or the stuff he removed from the trash?" Tex asked.

"The juicier one," Paul said. He rummaged through the bag he was carrying and pulled out a small folder, handing it to Tex who practically snatched it from his hand. He scanned the first page, eyebrows shooting up.

"You got anything else on this?" he asked.

"All the backstage things—IP addresses for the emails and all that stuff—are on the second page," supplied Paul.

Tex nodded, skimming the next page even as he stood. "Give me ten minutes," he said, strolling out the door.

"Does he believe us?" Carol asked.

"He's Tex. I don't pretend to read his mind. But the fact that he's taking us seriously is a good enough sign for me. But we'll have to wait and see."

Eleven minutes later, he sauntered back in, several new pages in his hand. Carol marked the mild irritation on his face.

"We traced the mystery email's IP address to one of the library computers," he explained. "As in, that's where they set it up. A couple of minutes before they sent that first email."

Paul nodded in understanding, his own frustration better masked than the sheriff's, but still evident.

"Meaning we aren't going to be able to figure out who actually set it up," Paul said. "The computers at the library are free to use. You don't need a membership."

"Which means it doesn't let your friend off the hook," Tex said.

"But it proves someone lured him here!" Carol argued. "And pointed him to that specific B&B. Harriet was terrified of James. Do you really think that she would bring him here?"

"She might if she thought she had found a way to rid herself of him for good," Tex countered, the logic grating at her. "Look, there's a strong chance you're right. This definitely puts everything in a new perspective, at the very least."

Carol huffed, opening her mouth to argue, but Paul reached out and took her gently by the elbow as he bent to whisper in her ear. "Let's take the victories where we can get them, all right?" he asked in a low whisper. He glanced up at Tex, who watched them with interest and worn patience. "Thanks, Tex," Paul said, giving a curt nod. "We'll let you know if we find anything else, all right?"

And he steered Carol out the door before she could argue further.

CHAPTER 15

Carol huffed, running her fingers through her hair as her mind spun. All her senses were pointing in one direction at the moment, but she had no hard proof. Her research suggested it. But beyond that, she hadn't uncovered anything concrete. She couldn't point the finger at someone without more.

"You're thinking something," Paul said, studying Carol. "You've got that annoyed concentration look you get when you're thinking about something that's bothering you."

She snorted. "I probably get that expression a lot, then," she quipped.

"You do," he confirmed, eyes sparkling. "So tell me what's bothering you."

"You know what's bothering me," she grumbled. "It's Tex and his dismissal of everything I say."

"He's not doing it out of malice," Paul pointed out reasonably. "He's doing what he thinks is best, because he has to follow the rules. So push that frustration and put it to good use somewhere else." He raised his eyebrows. "So where do you want to direct that frustration instead?"

Carol shot him a look. "I'm supposed to be the elder here," she shot back, earning her a shrug. Sighing, she closed her eyes, trying to channel the annoyance into something productive. She ran everything she had learned over the last couple of days. Several things didn't add up. She knew that. But pushing through the frustration, she tried to figure out the part that was bothering her.

"The bed-and-breakfast," she said, her brow furrowed. "I want to know why it was listed in that email. And I would like to know if Petra might have known about Harriet. Whoever did this knew who Harriet was and that she lived in town. Despite what she said, Petra might have lied about keeping tabs on Ratfield."

Paul nodded. "Then we should talk with her again," he said.

Carol's brow furrowed. "There's a chance she might not want to talk to us," Carol pointed out. "She didn't exactly like my brute force attempt to get answers the other day."

He pushed himself from his chair, grunting as he did. "We're not going to find out just sitting here," he said. "But let's take the car. I've got a couple of things that might help."

Paul never told her what he was talking about when he mentioned the car, and neither did he bring it up again when they pulled to a stop in front of the Seaport Bed and Breakfast. They clambered out, walking to the front door.

DEADLY FLASH FROM THE PAST

If Petra had been neutral to frosty the last time Carol stepped into the house, she was downright covered in ice this time. Carol could practically feel the warm summer air turn frigid against her bare shoulders.

"Absolutely not." Petra shot to her feet, glowering as she marched toward the two of them. "I want you out."

Paul held up his hands in a placating gesture. "Ms. Bedi, we're just trying to get the answers."

"Well, you're not getting them here," she snapped. She jabbed a finger at Carol. "You can turn around and walk out right now. I'm not going to sit here and let you accuse me of something I didn't do."

"Of course," Paul said, keeping his voice and expression neutral, everything about him the epitome of pleasant and unthreatening. "But I was hoping we could at least ask one question."

"No. Now get—"

"Do you know why your B&B was mentioned in an email to James Ratfield?" Paul asked. "The same email mentioning that his estranged wife lived in Whispering Haven?"

Her finger wavered, but stayed pointing at Paul. Her mouth opened and closed, but no words came out. Carol studied her, looking at her posture and her stricken features. She couldn't tell whether the surprise on her face was because this was news to her, or because she hadn't thought people would find out. Likewise, she couldn't tell if the panic flickering in her eyes was panic because someone had uncovered her secret, or because she was innocent and she understood the implications.

"No," she finally managed to say. "No."

Granted, if she had anything to do with it, or had done it herself, she would have said the same thing. Carol couldn't tell if she believed Petra or not. Glancing at Paul, she couldn't decide whether Paul believed her, either.

Whatever his actual thoughts might be, he seemed to be adopting a neutral stance, one that bordered on sympathetic to Petra. "Do you know anyone who might try to implicate you?" Paul asked.

Petra shook her head, her eyes wide with shock and fright. She took a deep breath, and once she had steadied herself, some of her fire seemed to come back.

"I don't know what the heck is going on," she said. Her hands trembled, and Carol couldn't tell if it was out of rage, or out of fear. "But I don't want any part of it. I want you out of here now."

"We're trying to help," Paul said. "If you know anything—"

"I don't," Petra snapped in a clipped voice that barely contained her anger. "Now leave. Before you make this any worse."

Carol waited for Paul to argue further. Instead, to her surprise, he simply nodded.

"Thank you for your time," he said. Spinning on his heels, he made his way back to the door, Carol hurrying after him, trying to catch up to his long stride.

"Well, that was a waste," Carol sighed as they stepped back out into the sunny day. "I probably shouldn't have been so aggressive that last time I was here."

DEADLY FLASH FROM THE PAST

"Probably not," Paul said mildly. He didn't sound particularly upset or even disappointed. His hands were stuffed in his pocket and he stared up at the sky, rocking back and forth as if lost in thought. If Carol had been expecting him to deny or refute the gloomy sentiment, she was out of luck. Before she could fire back a snarky retort, he said, "But I wouldn't feel too bad about it. I think we've still got a few avenues we could try." He gave her a smirk as he took in her bewilderment.

"Like what?"

He turned to look at her, his eyes sparkling. "You're forgetting a very important detail, you know," he said. "And I think it might help us."

Carol waited for him to continue. When he didn't, she folded her arms.

"I give up," she said, earning a chuckle from Paul.

"Trash day is tomorrow," he said, then sauntered toward his car. "I hope you brought gloves," he called over his shoulder.

"Gloves? Why?" It took Carol a minute. "Oh. Joy."

Paul, as if he had been prepared for this the entire time, pulled out two sets of gloves from his trunk, handing one pair to Carol. "I told you the car would come in handy," he said, winking. When they were certain no one was looking and that no one would question what they were about to do, they snuck around the side of the house, where they found two trash bins.

Wishing Paul had also thought to bring masks, or at least a clothespin, she flicked open one of the trashcans.

"What exactly are we trying to find?" she asked, keeping her voice low while also trying not to breathe in the stench of rotting food.

"Not sure yet," he admitted, also keeping his voice low as they rummaged through the trash. Every so often, he would pop up his head to keep an eye on the area, to make sure no one was coming. "We'll know if we find something."

She stopped, pulling her hand out of the trashcan to stare at him. "You mean you don't even know if there's something back here?" she asked.

He shrugged, then winked. "All part of the job."

Sighing, thinking she and Paul would have a long conversation about advanced warning when all of this was over, grumbled and turned back to dig through the trash, unsure of what she might find, if anything. She didn't know what to look for or what might—

She grabbed something.

She jerked her hand back. Slowly, heart thudding, she shifted away the last of the debris covering whatever it was she had just grabbed, knowing in her heart what it would be before she saw it.

"Paul," she breathed, eyes locked on the contents of the trashcan.

Paul must have noticed something in the tone of her voice, because the gentle rattling next to her ceased. A moment later, a shadow fell over her as Paul peered in the can. He stiffened as he took in what they were both seeing.

A pistol.

"I'm guessing that's a Walther PDP?" Carol asked, her voice going uncharacteristically soft.

"You guessed right," Paul confirmed. "And I'd bet my bottom dollar that its bullets are a match for the ones that killed James Ratfield."

"Should...should we move it?" Carol asked, more than a little relieved when Paul shook his head a second later.

"No need for that, I don't think," he declared. "I think it's best we keep it where it is and get the police over here ASAP."

She held up her camera. "Let's take a photo, just in case it gets moved."

Paul nodded. "Good thinking."

She snapped a photo; the pistol surrounded by bags of trash and old, stained containers. She wondered what would have happened had they not found it. Would the killer have gotten away?

"Let's go have a chat with the sheriff," Paul said, closing the trash can. "I have a funny feeling he's going to be very interested in what we just found."

CHAPTER 16

Tex listened to their story, skeptical at first, then intrigued, then alert. The more they told him, the edgier his body got, as if he was coiling himself, ready to spring into action. She could practically see the gears turning in his head.

"And you're sure about this?" he asked as they finished.

In answer, Carol tugged her camera strap off over her head and handed him the camera. "There's the picture," she said, then added, perhaps unnecessarily, "We didn't put it there ourselves."

Tex tilted his head, raising one eyebrow in amusement as he regarded Carol. "Never said you did," he replied simply. "Or even thought it, for that matter."

"Right," Carol muttered, heat flaring up her face.

He studied the picture for what felt like was longer than necessary. She waited, heart pounding, wondering what was going to happen next. Had they solved the case? Had they somehow made a grievous error and were about to be arrested themselves?

"Right." Tex handed the camera back to her. His face was inscrutable, but then he said. "You've got enough. That should convince a judge to get us an arrest warrant. Good job."

"Really?"

Carol had thought she would be elated, that she would feel a sense of accomplishment for identifying the killer and bringing him to justice. She had followed the clues and come up with the correct answer. She had helped solve a murder, and now that killer would be brought to justice.

Except, instead of triumph, the feeling that nestled deep inside her was unpleasant, sour, curdling her good mood. It took her a moment to realize that feeling was doubt mixed with guilt. Something, maybe it was her intuition, was telling her that something was wrong. That her theory was wrong. That the killer was wrong. Deep down, she didn't believe it was Petra.

The thought nearly sent her reeling backward as it slammed into her. She sucked in a breath. She couldn't understand it. Why, after everything, was she suddenly so certain she had gotten it wrong?

Something didn't add up, something she had missed in her haste and excitement. It took her a long moment to uncover what that might be, before it finally struck. Why on earth would Petra have told James Ratfield to come to her B&B, or all places? Surely she would have guessed how suspicious that would make her. She didn't seem like an unintelligent person. If she had been trying to cover her tracks, wouldn't she have listed a different place to stay? Or not listed one at all.

And the gun. Why would she throw it in her own trashcan? *Especially* if Ratfield stayed here. She would have known the police would come looking, and they would have had every right to hunt around in the trash if they so desired. There were far too many risks, too many variables, too many ways she might get caught. Why implicate herself like that?

Because she didn't do it, Carol thought, a chill speeding up her spine.

"Maybe we shouldn't do this," Carol muttered. "Maybe we should wait. Double check everything, you know?"

Tex gave her a perplexed, speculative look, brow creasing between his eyes. "We've got enough evidence to do something about it now," he said. "I would have thought you would be thrilled. This is what you wanted, right? Someone other than your friend?"

Carol shrugged, not looking at Tex, still mulling over the situation in her head. She wished she could squash the uncertainty creeping into her bones. Everything had been so easy an hour ago.

"I just don't want the wrong person arrested," she said.

"Well, if the information you just plopped in my lap is true, I think you've delivered the right person," Tex promised, gesturing at the file. "This is good stuff, you two."

"Happy to help," Paul said, even as his gaze turned to Carol. She could tell without looking that he sensed something was wrong, but when she didn't look back, he moved to readdress the sheriff.

"We've got to get a judge to sign off on a warrant," Tex said. "Which means I've gotta get going. Thanks again for bringing this in."

It was as polite a dismissal as possible. The two of them filed out. However, instead of the sweet taste of triumph she had been anticipating, all she felt was bitter guilt.

The guilt lasted through the night and into the next day.

She thought about it as she got ready for bed, as she woke up, as she fed Buttons, as she prepared her coffee, as she started gardening. It upset her so much that she couldn't even fret about her problem finding a gift for Sarah Jean. All she could think about was how wrong it all felt.

Finally, she couldn't take it any longer. She needed to talk to Petra. She needed to know more about what was going on. Pushing away from the table, she snatched her purse and her keys and hurried to her car. There was no time for walking today.

Except, car or no, it turned out she was already too late. Several police cars, their lights blinking red and blue as they cast their colors across the lawn and onto the cream-colored exterior of the house, lined the street in front of the bed-and-breakfast, and two more sat in the driveway. Carol jumped from her car and raced to the front, heart hammering even as she knew she was already too late.

"I swear, I don't know what you're talking about!" Petra exclaimed as Carol burst through the door. She could barely see the B&B owner surrounded by a cluster of officers. "I didn't realize who it was until several days later. He put down a fake name. See?" A rustle of paper, and Carol was certain Petra was flourishing a print out of Ratfield's reservation.

"So the fact that your bed-and-breakfast was mentioned in the anonymous email sent to him...that was a coincidence?" Carol heard Tex's voice ask, with no faint amount of skepticism.

"Yes!"

"Are you a member of the library, Ms. Bedi?"

"Of course. Because I love books. I don't see why that has anything to do with any of this."

The panic creeping into Petra's voice made Carol squirm with discomfort.

"That's where an email telling Redding about Harriet came from, one that mentioned your B&B."

Petra's eyes darted to Carol, then back to Tex. "I wouldn't be stupid enough to put my own B&B in an email. That would just come to point back at me."

"Sure, but you had a motive for killing him, and you would have known his comings and goings if he had been staying here."

"Motive?" Petra gave a high laugh that didn't quite mask the panicked desperation. "Look at me. I own this gorgeous house. I'm happy. Regardless of any inheritance I might have been denied, does it really look like I want for anything? I love it here. I love my life. Do you think I'm going to go out of my way to ruin it by getting revenge on a man I haven't seen since I was ten?"

Tex didn't respond to that. Instead, he pulled out a set of handcuffs. "Please put your hands behind your back, Ms. Bedi," Tex said.

Petra paled, but obeyed. Carol watched as the police handcuffed Petra and steered her toward one of the cars.

In one last, desperate act, she reached out and took Tex by the arm.

"I think we were wrong," Carol said, her voice low. "Look at her. Look how confused and shocked she is."

"Of course she's shocked," Tex responded. "She didn't expect to get caught."

Carol shook her head, eyes blazing with defiance. "We got the wrong person," she insisted. "I made a huge mistake."

Tex glowered, his expression set, lips straight and eyes slightly narrowed, the sternest she had seen him in a long time. He pulled his bicep from her grasp.

"Carol, I appreciate you want to get it right. And you have. The case is over."

"But—"

Tex interrupted her, holding up a hand. "If you want to accuse someone else, come back with more evidence," he said.

And he walked to the car, preparing to drive Petra away and to her fate.

CHAPTER 17

"I don't know who I'm angrier with," Carol said, pacing back and forth, her mug of tea on the island completely forgotten. "Tex, for not listening to me, or myself for getting it wrong in the first place."

"You followed the evidence," Paul pointed out from his chair. "Sometimes, that's all you can do."

"The evidence was wrong, though," Carol said. "Someone wanted to frame Petra. And unless we can find evidence that proves that, she's going to go to jail."

She paced back and forth, rubbing her head and muttering in frustration to herself. From her seat on top of the table, Buttons watched, her intelligent eyes tracking Carol's path with interest as her tail twitched. She gave a plaintive *meow* and hopped down, coming up to Carol and rubbing against her legs, weaving in and out as though trying to get her human to stop pacing. She glanced up, blinking at Carol with large eyes as if in question, wondering what on earth could have possibly upset her this much.

Giving a soft smile, temporarily mollified, Carol hoisted Buttons into her arm, cradling her like a baby. The cat purred and nestled snuggly against Carol's chest, giving her a fond look before closing her eyes and starting to fall asleep.

"It's not your fault," Paul said.

"It is, though." Carol sighed, scratching Button's belly as the feline began to doze. "I was the one who brought it all to Tex. I should have done more investigating first."

"It wasn't just you, remember?" Paul pointed out, sipping tea from his own mug.

Carol snorted, shaking her head. "If it were just you, you would have figured out what was going on in a heartbeat. You'd have done more research before going to Tex."

"Pretty sure I was the one who said we should go see him in the first place," Paul pointed out. "It's not your fault."

"Yes, it is!" Carol groaned, rubbing her temples. "I'm as bad a detective as I am a friend! I still can't think of a single thing to get Sarah Jean."

"That doesn't make you a bad friend, either," Paul said. "It just means your friend is impossible to shop for. Which she is. I've known Sarah Jean a lot longer than you have. She's *always* been like this. You not being able to figure out a gift for her isn't a failing on your part, Carol. You have to understand that."

Carol sniffed, but didn't say anything. She took a deep breath, squeezing her cat tight against her as she forced her brain to slow down, for her mind to relax enough for her to get a grip on the situation and figure out the next steps. Buttons' warm presence, the smell of her fur, and the reassuring way her purr vibrated through Carol began to soothe her, and after a long moment, she was finally able to think a bit straighter.

"We've got to make sure one way or the other," Carol said.

"I agree." Paul stood, stretching. "It sounds as though you might have an idea on what to do next."

Carol nodded as she turned everything over in her mind. "I want to go talk to Harriet and Eric again," she said.

He bobbed his head up and down, as if it was what he had been expecting. He drained the rest of his drink in three large gulps.

"In that case, that's exactly what we're going to do," Paul said, smacking his lips. "Come on, let's get a move on. No time to waste."

Harriet flung her arms around Carol the instant the door opened.

"Carol! I can't thank you enough!" Harriet squealed as she tightened the embrace, practically squeezing all the air out of Carol.

Don't thank me just yet, Carol thought, returning the hug. *I may be locking up your boyfriend here in a bit.*

"How are you doing?" Carol asked.

"Better now," Harriet said, her eyes still sparkling. She took a deep, shaking breath. "I can't believe it's finally over with. It's been a wild ride, you know?"

"Yeah," Carol said. "I do."

"Come on in. Both of you." Harriet seemed to just now notice Paul standing behind Carol. She beamed, eyes crinkling, before jerking Carol inside by the wrist.

Eric stood when the trio entered the living room. He gave a broad grin.

"Man, I owe you two a huge debt." He pulled Carol into a bear hug, then broke away to shake Paul's hand. "I don't know what we would have done without you."

She studied Eric, trying to find any hint that he might have something to do with Ratfield's death. He certainly loved Harriet enough to make sure she was safe. But would he lure Ratfield to Whispering Haven, potentially putting Harriet at risk? And their alibis lined up with one another, meaning that, if Eric had murdered James, then Harriet had been complicit.

Looking at the two of them, Carol struggled to reconcile the idea that Eric was a cold-blooded killer. The way he looked now spoke only of relief, not of triumph.

"I'm glad we were able to help," Carol said.

"Honestly, it feels weird feeling relief for bringing James Ratfield's killer to justice," Eric said. "I would have been on their side if it weren't for Harriet getting blamed." He winced. "Is that bad?"

"I think it's reasonable," Paul said. "He wasn't the nicest person."

DEADLY FLASH FROM THE PAST

Harriet sighed, slumping into a chair. "I still can't believe he killed a woman," she admitted. "I actually looked into it, after you came to talk to me. I thought there was no way it was the truth. And yet..." She shivered, taking a deep breath. "Yeah...I had to realize you were right."

"I'm sorry," Carol said. "I know how hard that must be."

Harriet shrugged, suddenly looking years older. "I did some research into the woman. It's heartbreaking. Did you know that she was about to get married?"

Carol's head whipped up. Beside her, Paul stiffened to attention as well.

"Really?" Carol asked. "I didn't see that anywhere."

Harriet nodded.

"Did it say who?" Carol asked, barely breathing now as connections slowly snapped into place, her eyes growing wide as saucers as a distant memory resurfaced, dragging new implications along with it.

Harriet shook her head, a little glumly. "Sadly, no. Seems like he wanted to keep his name out of the spotlight."

Fumbling with her phone, much to Paul and Harriet and Eric's bewilderment, she hastily pulled up her search browser and typed in two names: Alexandra Gibson and Derrick Redding.

"I don't believe it," Carol whispered, eyes locked on the phone as her brain spun in disbelief.

"What?" the rest of the room asked in unison.

In response, Carol held out her phone, showing the small blurb listed in a small paper in Illinois.

"The Gibson family proudly announces the engagement of their daughter, Alexandra, to Derrick Redding," Paul read. His mouth dropped open as he stared at the photo of the happy couple beneath the announcement. "Is that who I think it is?" he asked.

Carol bobbed her head up and down. She and Paul shot to their feet. Carol's heart thundered with excitement and adrenaline as the final pieces of the puzzle fell into place.

"Harriet, I'm so sorry, but we have to go." The dazzling grin rather diminished the impact of the apology.

"Oh, all right," Harriet said. "Is everything all right?"

"Everything is brilliant," Carol promised, still grinning. "But we've got to run! Bye!"

She and Paul raced out the door, leaving behind a bewildered Harriet and Eric staring after them.

"Are you thinking what I'm thinking?" Carol asked, breathless with exhilaration.

Paul grinned, turning to look at Carol with a mock speculative look on his face. He rubbed his chin as if deep in thought. "I think it's time we had another chat with Mr. Redding, and see if he has a better idea of where his gun might have gone, don't you?"

CHAPTER 18

The cool night breeze carried the faint taste of salt as Carol and Paul hurried down the street, their feet pounding against the cobblestone that covered the main line of shops. Streetlamps flickered on, joining the moon to illuminate the area.

Despite the growing lateness of the hour, a few shops remained lit, and couples still wandered. Several paused and watched with bemused interest as Paul and Carol charged toward the art store, hoping they wouldn't be too late.

They were in sight of the store, its wide windows displaying sea-themed portraits and sculptures, when the lights inside flicked off. They slowed as they neared, a familiar-looking figure closing the door behind himself, before turning to lock it.

From this distance and angle, a new flash of recognition struck Carol like a lightning bolt. She sucked in a breath, nearly losing her footing as their sprint turned into a walk.

In this light, he looked exactly like the man who had been following James Ratfield the day he died.

She wanted to warn Paul, to give him the head's up that the person he was about to be dealing with could be even more dangerous than they had thought. Before she could get the words out of her mouth, Paul had already taken several steps ahead of Carol. She couldn't see his face, but she could imagine it set in determination.

"Derrick," he called, just as Carol opened her mouth to warn him of her new revelation.

Derrick blinked in polite bemusement as he looked between the two of them. Something like dislike or fear flickered behind his eyes, but that was the only indication that he sensed something was wrong.

Paul came to a stop a few feet away from Derrick. She noticed he was just far enough to stay out of arm's reach, while staying close enough to remain within striking distance, should the need arise.

If Derrick noticed this, he didn't give any indication. "Can I help you?" he asked politely. "If you want some art for your friend, I'm afraid I'm closed for the day."

"I'm not here about that this time. I wanted to ask you a few questions about your fiancé," Carol responded, folding her arms. "Alexandra Gibson?"

Derrick took a half-step back, but that was the only indication he gave that the accusation had unsettled him. He gave a humorless laugh as he looked between her and Paul. "Alexandra *who*?" he demanded.

"Gibson," Paul responded.

"Now, really." He looked at Carol and shook his head in sympathy before turning to Paul. "I don't know what she's told you, but she's clearly not in her right mind."

He chuckled, but Paul didn't join in. Instead, he pulled out his phone. "So, to be clear, you're not the Derrick Redding mentioned in Alexandra Gibson's engagement notice here?" he asked.

Derrick shrugged. "Probably a lot of Derrick Redding's in the world," he said.

"And this isn't you with her in a photo?" Paul asked, flipping to a photo and holding it to him.

Derrick's Adam's apple bobbed up and down as he studied the photo, his expression blank even as his face drained of color. He glanced up at Paul, who continued to stare him down, unsmiling. Finally, he seemed to give in.

"Yeah. That's me. How'd you know about Alexandra?" he asked.

"There was a photo of a woman on the wall in your house," Carol explained. "I assumed a family member. When I saw Alexandra's photo in the paper, I thought she looked familiar. It wasn't until a few other things clicked into place that I realized where I'd seen it before. Alexandra was the woman I saw in the photo."

Derrick nodded, heaving a sigh as though suddenly a hundred years older.

"All right, yeah, Alexandra was my fiancé," he said. His expression turned soft, a nostalgic smile spreading across his face. "She was incredible. Just a wonderful woman, you know? Smart, funny..."

"What happened to her?" Paul asked, stuffing his hands in his pockets. He adopted a concerned, unassuming expression. He resembled the type of person you might vent all your troubles to at a bar.

Except Derrick didn't seem to trust it. His eyes narrowed, and he folded his arms. He shifted his stance. Carol stiffened, her attention drawn to his hip, where a lump appeared to lurk beneath his shirt. She opened her mouth, preparing to warn Paul. But a moment later, Derrick shifted again, and the lump vanished. Her shoulders relaxed.

Just a trick of the light, she told herself.

The hostility ebbed out of Derrick. He sighed, slumping against the window. "She got in a car accident," he said. "Her car stalled on the highway. Nothing to be done."

"I'm sorry for your loss," Paul said. He regarded Derrick, keeping an eye on the man. "And I'm guessing you know James Ratfield, the man who died by your gun, is the one who sold your fiancé the car that killed her."

He nodded. "No use denying it, is there?" he asked. "No idea he was in town. When I heard the name of the guy who died, I was shocked. Was positive it was a weird coincidence. At least until I saw a photo of the guy."

"So what happened after Alexandra died?" Paul asked.

"Once the trial was over, I left Chicago and wandered around for a few months. Showed up here and decided to settle down. I fell in love with the area."

Paul nodded, still keeping that friendly demeanor even as he continued fixing the trap around Derrick.

DEADLY FLASH FROM THE PAST

"It's certainly an incredible area. What do you like about the place?" he asked, raising an eyebrow.

Derrick chortled. "What's not to like?" he asked. "I like just about everything. The fresh sea air, the delicious food, the tranquility, the view, the people..."

"What about the library?" Carol asked.

He stiffened.

"I mean, it seems like a fine place," he said. "But I don't know much about it."

"Really?" Carol feigned confusion. She tapped her chin, glancing over at Paul. "That's weird. Because, Paul, you have a friend who works at the library, don't you?"

"I do." Paul nodded in confirmation. "I gave her a call on our way over here. I asked her if there were any regulars. She said you've been coming in quite a lot lately. I asked her what it was you were doing, and she said you typically spent some time on the computer. What were you doing there, I wonder?"

Derrick straightened, eyes narrowing as his gaze darted between the two of them. Folding his arms, he said, "I don't know what you're getting at, but I think you two are starting to be nuisances. I'd suggest you two get out of here before I call the cops."

Paul chuckled, unsettling Derrick. "I don't think you want the police coming here," he said. He turned to Carol. "Do you?"

Carol shook her head. "I think that sounds like a horrible idea," she agreed.

Derrick laughed. When neither of the others joined in, he sobered. His gaze darted between Carol and Paul.

"What on earth are you talking about?" he demanded.

"Well, the instant the cops get here, we'll tell them you killed James Ratfield," Carol said.

CHAPTER 19

Derrick stared; mouth slightly open. Then he laughed, the sound echoing on the now-deserted street as the last of the shops closed and people trickled away.

"You're joking, right?" he asked.

"Of course not," Paul said. "You killed Ratfield with your gun, and you pretended it had been stolen the day before, so the police wouldn't think you had anything to do with it."

Derrick sobered. His gaze darted between Carol and Paul. She could feel his gaze drilling into her, as if trying to decide how much they really knew, and how much was simply conjecture.

He must have determined they had nothing, because a second later, he shook his head, giving a soft chuckle. His shoulders, tense a second earlier, eased. "You guys are nuts," he said. "I don't know what it is you think you know, but it's wrong. Besides, what about that bed-and-breakfast woman?

Petra? Her whole family had a grudge against James Ratfield."

"Which you used to your advantage," Paul added. He folded his arms. "How thrilled were you when you found that connection? And when Harriet came to town, for that matter?"

Derrick shook his head, taking a step back and folding his arms as he glowered at the duo.

"You two are absolutely nuts," Derrick sneered. "Lunatics who are harassing me for no reason. They've already arrested the killer. They found the gun in the trash outside her house, for crying out loud."

Paul's lips curled into a triumphant smirk. He tilted his head as he studied Derrick. "And how would you know that?" he asked.

Alarm flickered across Derrick's face for a moment before he adopted a mask of composure again. He shrugged. "Tex told me when he gave me back the gun," he said.

Paul was already shaking his head. "Tex hasn't given you that gun back yet," he said. "And the police are keeping the trash bit under wraps as well. The only way you would have known that would have been if you were the one who put it there."

Derrick scoffed, rolling his eyes. "You know that things never stay secret in Whispering Haven for long," he argued. "I must have gotten it wrong. I think it was Fiona who told me."

"And how did Fiona know?" Carol retorted. Derrick shot her a furious glower, filled with spite and dislike.

DEADLY FLASH FROM THE PAST

"How should I know? You probably blabbed to her," he said.

Paul's smirk vanished, replaced by a scowl as he stared down Derrick.

"If you're going to try that line, you're going to need a better scapegoat," he said. "I know Carol well enough to know she wouldn't tell anyone something the police ordered her to keep secret."

"You're going to believe a dithering old lady over me?" he asked.

"Absolutely," Paul said. "Especially considering she's neither dithering or old."

A rush of warmth and gratitude flooded over Carol, but she kept her attention focused on the situation at hand. She could tell by the way Derrick's eyes flicked back and forth, as though looking for an escape route as his body coiled to run, that they were on the right path. They just needed to push a little more.

"My guess is that you were watching Ratfield like a hawk," she said. "Ever since he disappeared from Chicago. He really should have changed his name. There are notices of Harriet and Ratfield in police reports, so it would be easy to figure out who she was. Same with Petra. If you do a bit of research, you can figure out who her family is and how Ratfield screwed them over. How long did it take to figure out who they were, and then put the plan into action?"

"Petra got here first," Paul said. "My bet was he knew he could maybe use her, but didn't know how. And then Harriet came to town. Once he recognized who she was, he put together everything he needed. He waited a while to make sure he had covered all his bases. But he didn't do it well enough. The missing gun is what gave you away. There were too many questions that we couldn't answer."

Derrick shook his head, half laughing, as if Paul had just said the funniest joke in the world. Paul's eyes narrowed, shoulders tensing, as if sensing a shift in the situation.

Derrick eyes Carol and Paul, as if appraising them, or perhaps really seeing them for the first time, his head cocked.

"All right, so maybe you figured out more than I gave you credit for," he said. "Maybe I did leave too many questions. Except you forgot one crucial one that you really should have asked."

Carol and Paul exchanged glances as unease prickled up Carol's spine. Her mouth had gone dry. They turned back to Derrick.

"What question is that?" Carol asked.

Derrick gave a sinister, blood-curdling grin. "You probably should have asked if I had any other guns."

Too late, Carol realized their mistake. Derrick's hand dropped to his waist, flying back up a moment later holding a gun.

Carol froze. Paul didn't.

"Run!" he exclaimed.

They bolted down the street, heading toward the center of town. Carol's head darted first one way, then the other. The streets remained deserted, shop lights off. How was there no one around?

She didn't have time to ponder their bad luck. Footsteps pounded behind them, and Carol could just picture Derrick speeding toward them, his gun raised as he leveled it at one of them—

A gunshot rang out. Something whizzed past Carol's ear and she shrieked. She wanted to freeze up in fear, but forced herself to keep going, knowing that if she stopped, she wouldn't be as lucky next time.

"Split up," Paul panted next to her. "He won't be able to get both of us. I'll try to make sure he follows me and not you."

Carol nodded, a stitch growing in her side. She peeled away, darting down a side alley while Paul continued straight. She pushed forward despite the fact that her side ached and her legs were beginning to grumble in protest.

If I make it out of this, I promise I'll start working out more, she thought. Except the sounds of growing footsteps and ragged breathing behind her told her that Paul's attempt to lure Derrick away from Carol hadn't worked. The murderer had decided to follow her instead.

Carol wasn't going to let that phase her, though. She needed to keep pushing forward. She continued to race ahead, even as she knew she couldn't keep it up for much longer. If she wasn't able to lose him soon, she was a dead woman.

Despite living here for a year, some of the streets remained unfamiliar to her. She had no idea where she was, her mental map of the area warping and distorting. She turned a corner, certain it would lead to an open street...

Only to wind up staring at the brick wall of a dead-end alley.

She came to a halt, eyes widening with horror as the footsteps closed the distance. By the time she spun back around, Derrick stood in the mouth of the alley, blocking her only escape route, and she knew her luck had run out.

He held up the gun, eyes squinting as he aimed. There was nowhere for her to go. She was stuck in the alley, looking down the barrel of a pistol. She sucked in a breath.

"You're not going to get away with this," Carol declared, even as her heart pounded and she had a hard time believing the words. "Paul's going to report this to the police and they'll be after you in no time."

Derrick shrugged, keeping the pistol trained on her. "I'll find him after I'm done with you," he said. "And if I don't, then I'll run. They might chase me for a bit, but they'll give up, eventually."

"And if they catch you?" Carol asked.

Another shrug. "Then at the very least, I'll have avenged Alexandra." His eyes narrowed. "But I'm not giving in without a fight."

Carol pressed her back against the brick wall, closing her eyes as she knew the end was coming. She waited for the tell-tale sound of a gunshot before blackness.

One heartbeat. Two.

Except, instead of a gunshot, she heard a loud *oof*, followed by a shuffle and the sound of something heavy thumping to the alley floor. Scuffling followed.

DEADLY FLASH FROM THE PAST

Frowning, sensing something had changed, Carol cracked one eye open. Both flew open as she registered the sight in front of her.

Paul had pinned Derrick to the ground. The gun had skittered away and now lay against the brick wall. Derrick snarled and thrashed as he tried to worm his way out from underneath the other man. Except Paul appeared unphased. He flipped Derrick over, pulling his arms behind his back and holding them there as he fished around for something in his pocket. A second later, Paul produced a handful of zip ties. He looped one around Derrick's wrists and cinched it tight. Once Derrick, furious and spitting venom at Paul and Carol, had been subdued, Paul glanced up at Carol.

"You all right?" Paul asked.

Carol nodded, slumping against the back wall as her heart went to her chest.

"Just give me a minute to make sure I'm not having a heart attack," she joked, still panting. She cracked a half grin. "After all, I am just a dithering old lady."

Paul flashed a grin back at her, then hauled Derrick to his feet.

"Come on," Paul said. "I think Tex is going to want to have a word with you."

He pulled Derrick out of the alley and out onto the main street, heading toward the police station while Carol followed behind.

CHAPTER 20

Two days later, Carol and Sarah Jean sat at Carol's house, chatting over a cup of tea. Buttons slept between them on the table, paw thrown over her nose.

"I'm annoyed with you, by the way," Sarah Jean said, folding her arms in mock sternness.

Carol stiffened. "What? Why?"

"I had to hear from Fiona of all people that not only did you and Paul get Derrick arrested, but that he *pointed a gun at you*." Sarah Jean's eyes narrowed as she scrutinized her friend.

Carol's mouth dropped open. "How on earth did Fiona learn that?" She marveled. "Tex told us to keep it under wraps for the time being, and I know Paul wouldn't tell anyone."

"I told you. That woman has a superpower. She can sniff out gossip from a mile away." Sarah Jean's face crumpled, a mix of genuine concern and hurt on her face. "When were you going to tell me?"

"Sorry," Carol said, and genuinely meant it. "Though, in my defense, how on earth am I supposed to explain that story? And Tex did ask us to keep it quiet."

"Why? I would assume it wouldn't be an issue. It's not as though he isn't guilty if he pulled a gun on you. I don't see the need to keep it a secret."

"I think Tex wants to keep it hush hush to avoid more scandal," Carol said. "Plus, Derrick and his lawyer are trying to blame us. They're saying we accosted him and the whole thing was justified self defense."

Sarah Jean gaped. "That *jerk*," she hissed. "He's lucky he's behind bars, or he'd have me to deal with."

"Tex said that it shouldn't matter. They found some evidence at his house, and it's Paul's and my word against his. But he wants to make sure no one accidentally compromises the investigation until more things are in place."

"He did make sure that the town knows Harriet has nothing to do with it, at least," Sarah Jean said. "I heard him yesterday talking in town about how she was no longer a suspect. It definitely seemed like he was doing his best to make sure she wasn't going to have any trouble with the rest of town."

"Good," Carol said, sighing. "That's good. I had a brief chat with her yesterday. I'm glad everything is going to work out for her and Eric. And now that James is gone, she won't have to look over her shoulder anymore."

"I also heard that Harriet is going to have some money coming her way," Sarah Jean said. "According to Fiona, Harriet's still the main beneficiary of his will. He never changed it after the divorce. So all that money is coming her way."

"How on earth does she know that?" Carol asked.

Sarah Jean shrugged. "No idea. But if Fiona says it, then it's probably true. I wonder how Petra will feel about that, since she could argue it belongs to her in the first place."

Carol shrugged. "I guess we'll have to see. But I get the feeling she wasn't lying when she said she didn't care."

"I guess only time will tell," her friend said speculatively. Her eyes sharpened, honing in on Carol. "Except you're avoiding the real problem."

"What's that?" Carol asked, genuinely confused.

"You haven't told me what happened!" She tutted with mock consternation, adopting a playful scolding tone. "Now spill the details or we'll have a real problem."

Carol laughed, the sound reverberating through the house, causing Buttons to raise her head at the sound, before laying back on the table.

"Fair enough," Carol said. "All right, I'll try to do the story justice. Though I'm sure Fiona's is far more interesting."

Sarah Jean listened with rapt attention, her mouth forming a perfect 'o' that grew larger and larger with every word of Carol's tale.

"Wow," Sarah Jean finally said. Then another, "Wow."

Carol nodded, sipping on her tea, reaching out to scratch Buttons between the ears as she waited for Sarah Jean to process the story.

"That had to be terrifying," Sarah Jean said. "I couldn't imagine going through all that. I probably would have had a heart attack before he pulled the trigger."

"Honestly, it was a near miss," Carol admitted. "I'm pretty sure I saw my life flashing before my eyes until Paul tackled him."

"Well, for the record, I'm glad he stopped Derrick before he added another murder to his list," Sarah Jean said. "I would have been very upset if something would have happened to you."

"I'm sure you would have avenged me," Carol retorted, winking.

"Without a doubt! Derrick would have robbed me of the second-best gardener in town—myself being the first, of course. I wouldn't have had anyone to trade flowers with. I'd have had a few choice words for him if anything had happened to you."

"I'm sure you would have found someone else to chat gardens with in no time," Carol replied, even as a warmth spread through her body. She didn't know what she would do without Sarah Jean in town.

Sarah flapped her hand dismissively. "Sure, but it wouldn't be the same. Oh! I meant to tell you. I have some friends who are interested in the seed swap! They all love the idea. They're already talking about what they would be willing to trade for what, and what to do for out of season plants."

DEADLY FLASH FROM THE PAST

"That's wonderful!" Carol said. "I'll be looking forward to getting my hands on some of those calla lily seeds of Abigail's." She glanced at Buttons affectionately, reaching out to give her scratches behind the ears. "Though I'll have to make sure to keep Buttons away from them."

"I can give you a few tips," Sarah Jean responded. "I've had cats before who always seemed interested in trying to eat things that were terrible for them."

"I'd love that. Though I'll also have to deal with the fact that your garden is going to be even more glorious and you're going to be too busy tending to it. I can just imagine you hopping all around your yard tending to all the new plants."

"We'll see." Sarah Jean gave a rueful smile. "I may not be able to hop around as much, but I'm another year older today. I'm not the spring chicken I was yesterday."

Carol smirked. "Gee, is it your birthday? I must have forgotten. I'm so sorry. Let me see if there's something I can give that will make it up to you."

She stood, that smile still on her face, and she hurried to the fridge, humming to herself as she pulled out an elegant pale blue cake box.

Sarah Jean squeaked, hand going to her heart. "Carol, you didn't," she said, her face filled with affection.

"I did. I figured half of my gift would be not baking the cake myself," Carol joked, winking. "I picked it up from that cute bakery in town that you always rave about."

Sarah Jean beamed, clapping her hands together as Carol flipped the box open to reveal an elegant cake with the words *Happy Birthday Sarah Jean!* piped in elegant green buttercream.

"Is it what flavor I think it is?" Sarah Jean asked.

"If you mean coffee and caramel, then of course. I also think they went to extra trouble when they found out it was for you," Carol added. "They told me they added an extra layer for free."

"This is so sweet, Carol—no pun intended—thank you so much!" Sarah Jean hopped to her feet and wrapped her friend in a hug.

"Of course. You've looked out for me since I moved here. This is the least I can do." Carol's lip curled upward. "So it's a good thing I didn't stop there." At Sarah Jean's questioning glance, Carol held up a finger and strolled into the living room, returning moments later with a gift bag with pink tissue paper poking out of the top.

"You didn't have to do all this," Sarah Jean said.

"You're my friend. I wanted to." Still, her heart pounded a little as she held out the bag. "I really hope you like them."

Sarah Jean pulled out a picture frame, with a photo of her and Carol from their hiking trip a few weeks ago, their faces smushed together. Then she pulled out a set of seeds.

"You'll have to be careful with those," Carol said, giving a smirk. "They're rare, and they can be a bit particular about where they grow."

Sarah Jean gasped. "These aren't lily-of-the-valley seeds, are they?" she asked. "I've been trying to get my hands on them for ages."

"They are," Carol said.

"Wow...Just...wow." Her friend stared in wonder at the bag of seeds. "Thank you!"

"Do you like them?" Carol asked, still nervous.

"Like them? I love them!" Sarah Jean's eyes crinkled with delight. "But the best part about it is that it's from you. It's perfect."

She stood and wrapped her arms around Carol. "Thank you so much."

Carol smiled, hugging her friend tighter. Then she caught sight of movement on the counter, and her eyes widened as she let go of Sarah Jean. "Buttons, no!" She scooped up the grey cat right before her nose poked into the frosting of the cake.

"Guess flowers aren't the only thing I have to watch out for when it comes to Buttons," Carol joked, scratching the cat beneath the chin as Buttons purred against her.

"She has good taste, then," Sarah Jean responded. "Speaking of, I want a taste of this cake!"

She grabbed a knife, slicing two thick slices of cake and passing one to Carol after she deposited Buttons on the floor. And the two of them ate, chatting even as Carol wondered what lay in store for her next.

The End

Afterword

Thank you for reading ***Deadly Flash from the Past***. I really hope you enjoyed reading it as much as I had writing it!

If you have a minute, please consider leaving a review on Amazon or the retailer where you got it.

Many thanks in advance for your support!

FRAMED IN MISCHIEF

CHAPTER 1 SNEAK PEEK

The camera shutter gave a satisfying click as Carol snapped another photo. She tilted her head as she considered the picture she had just taken. The lighting wasn't quite right. She moved a bit to the right and took another photo. She nodded in satisfaction as she checked her work.

As she snapped another few photos, a man nearing fifty sauntered out of the newly built restaurant, The Sailing Captain, and over to Carol.

"How're things going?" Rick asked.

"So far, so good," Carol said. "I'm sure I've got some good photos in the mix that you can use."

Rick beamed. "Atta girl! I appreciate that." He clapped her on the back. "Hey, how about a couple with me in it? Make the restaurant look even better, right?"

"That's up to you," Carol said. "You're the one paying."

Rick cracked a charming grin. "Excellent." He ran a finger through his brown hair—obviously dyed—as he smoothed it out. He winked at Carol. "Don't worry. The camera loves me. Just do what you've been doing and they'll turn out great."

Pursing her lips, Carol glanced down at the camera, not saying anything. She was grateful for Rick taking a chance on her and offering her the job of photographing his restaurant before it opened in a couple of weeks. But Rick himself was beginning to grate on her, even though she had only been here for an hour, and she wondered if she shouldn't add a surplus charge for 'Unpleasant Personality.'

Still, she'd promised to do the job, and she intended to see it through. It wouldn't take much longer.

Rick struck a rather ridiculous pose that he clearly imagined was suave.

"Do you maybe want to stand like this?" Carol mimed a more relaxed, at ease pose.

"Nah, this is perfect," Rick said. "Come on, while the light is good."

"The customer is always right," Carol mumbled to herself. She readied her camera, already running through how she could edit the photo later to make the photo look better. She took a photo, and—

"There you are! I've been looking for you, you snake."

Carol's head whipped around, brow furrowed in confusion as a man marched toward them. He was bristling with anger as his eyes locked on Rick. He barely noticed Carol as he brushed past her to stomp up to Rick, stopping only when he was within arm's reach.

Rick blinked, cracking a charming grin even as he removed his hands from his pockets and unease flickered in his eyes.

"Heya, Will," Rick said. "How can I help you?"

Will didn't answer. Instead, he said, "What's this I hear about tearing it down?"

"What? The land you sold me?"

"Not the land—the restaurant on top of it. You know, the one you promised you wouldn't tear down? Funny how, when I walked by it the other day, I saw a bunch of demolition equipment. Stopped to ask one of the guys what was going on, and you know what he told me?"

Rick yawned, as if unconcerned by the man in front of him who looked ready to throw a punch. "I'm guessing you're going to tell me no matter what I say."

"He said the new owner is tearing it down to build a seaside hotel." Will folded his arms. "When you told me you wanted that land, you said it was so that you could help revitalize that restaurant. It's the only reason I sold to you. You didn't mention anything about a hotel in any of our chats."

Rick shrugged. "I changed my mind. I'm allowed to do that."

Will gritted his teeth. "It was in the contract." He snapped.

"Is it?" Rick tapped his chin, giving an infuriating grin. "Because, if I remember correctly-"

"What's going on, exactly?" Carol inquired, stepping up.

Will turned to look at her, then blinked, as if surprised she was even here.

"This jerk came to me a few weeks ago," Will snapped, gesturing at Rick with disgust. "Offering to buy some land that's been in my family for years. I've been short for cash, so I said yes. With the agreement that he wouldn't do anything to the businesses on top of it. They've been there for years and my family has always leased the land to those people. I didn't want their lives getting uprooted because I sold. Except today, I got a call from the tenant who runs the restaurant. She told me that the new owner had ordered her to vacate because they were tearing it all down. I didn't believe it, so I walked by."

Rick snorted, folding his arms and rolling his eyes. "You can't seriously be upset," he said. "You sold the land."

"We had an agreement."

"Get it in writing next time," Rick said. "Better make sure the contract is more explicit. There's nothing in there saying I couldn't tear down the buildings."

"Because you told me we wouldn't need it!" Will's eyes blazed with fire. His fingers clenched and unclenched as he glowered at the impassive Rick.

Carol, for her part, felt frozen to the spot, mouth partly open as she watched the exchange. She could practically feel the waves of rage radiating off Will. But what disconcerted her more was the smug, self-satisfied smirk on Rick's face. She glanced down at the camera clutched in her hand, as if trying to confirm something real and solid, to tell herself this was actually happening.

"I'd leave now, Will," Rick said, the smirk fading. "Before you do something you regret. Just remember that I can sue you to an oblivion if you keep pushing. I have way more resources than you."

Will's fingers curled. Rick noticed and laughed. "Go ahead, punch me."

Will stayed rooted to the spot, quivering with anger. Finally, he said, "This isn't over."

"Yes, it is," Rick retorted. He made a shooing motion. "Go before this gets any worse for you."

Glowering, but clearly admitting defeat, Will spun around, marching away. Carol and Rick watched, Carol's disbelief growing, until the man disappeared around a corner.

"Crazy guy," Rick muttered, shaking his head and giving a soft tut of sympathy. "My guess would be he has some anger issues to sort through. Or he needs to get adjusted to the real world." He shrugged, letting the incident roll off his back like water off a duck, then gave that same charming grin. "So, what do you say we start taking photos of the interior? You think I put a lot of effort into the outside? You haven't seen anything yet."

Carol didn't move. She remained frozen, stupefied as she stared at Rick. Rage and disgust washed over her as Rick looked expectantly at her.

"Well? Are you coming?"

Carol's jaw clamped shut. She glowered at Rick as she straightened, finally getting her bearings.

"No, I'm not," she said. "I don't work for crooks."

Rick laughed, eyes crinkling, sobering only when he noticed she hadn't joined in. "Seriously?" he asked. "You believe that guy? He's just upset because he thinks he got a bad deal and is gunning for more money."

"Sounded to me like you cheated him out of seaside property," Carol contradicted, her anger continuing to bubble as it grew hotter and hotter. "And he found out."

Rick snorted, shaking his head. "You're as crazy as he is," he said, his tone patronizing.

"And you're nothing more than a two-bit con-artist," Carol declared. "I'm going to make sure everyone knows it."

She spun around and marched down the street. As she did, she jammed her hand into her pocket, yanking out her phone. There were two people she could confidently rely on to spread this as far and wide as possible. The first was her best friend, Sarah Jean.

The second was the notorious town gossip, and that was whose number she punched into her phone with more aggression than strictly necessary.

"Fiona?" Carol said when the other end picked up. "Have I got some news for you."

Get your copy at all good retailers.

WHISPERING HAVEN COZY MYSTERY

Framed in Mischief

RUTH BAKER

Also by Ruth Baker

THE IVY CREEK COZY MYSTERY SERIES

Which Pie Goes with Murder? (Book 1)

Twinkle, Twinkle, Deadly Sprinkles (Book 2)

Eat Once, Die Twice (Book 3)

Silent Night, Unholy Bites (Book 4)

Waffles and Scuffles (Book 5)

Cookie Dough and Bruised Egos (Book 6)

A Sticky Toffee Catastrophe (Book 7)

Dough Shall Not Murder (Book 8)

Deadly Bites on Winter Nights (Book 9)

A Juicy Steak Tragedy (Book 10)

Southern Fried and Grief Stricken (Book 11)

Poisoned Freebies at Phoebe's (Book 12)

Tasty Edibles, Nasty Rumblings (Book 13)

A Spicy Side of Homicide (Book 14)

The Wedding Cake Conundrum (Book 15)

THE WHISPERING HAVEN COZY MYSTERY SERIES

Gone in a Snap (Book 1)

Say Cheese and Die Laughing (Book 2)

Deadly Flash from the Past (Book 3)

Framed in Mischief (Book 4)

Blurred Lines, Clear Crimes

Snap, Crackle and a Deadly Plot

Flash of Deceit

Newsletter Signup

Want **FREE** COPIES OF FUTURE **CLEANTALES** BOOKS, FIRST NOTIFICATION OF NEW RELEASES, CONTESTS AND GIVEAWAYS?

GO TO THE LINK BELOW TO SIGN UP TO THE NEWSLETTER!

https://cleantales.com/newsletter/

Printed in Great Britain
by Amazon